"We need four men to drive two trucks loaded with nitroglycerine up to Poza Rica. Only experienced drivers willing to risk their lives can do it. No one else should apply."

It was a job nobody wanted. "We're not crazy," the local workers grumbled as they moved away from the company representative making the announcement.

But four men who watched and listened considered the offer. Victor was evading the French authorities who wanted to arrest him for fraud. Jackie was scheduled to be hit by the Mafia. Kassem's bombing activities had the Israelis on his trail. Nilo had put distance between himself and his past for reasons he alone knew.

So they signed on, these four, for a mission only the most hopeless could hope to complete.

SORCERER

A novel by
John Minahan

Based on the
screenplay by
Walon Green

Based on the novel
"The Wages of Fear" by
Georges Arnaud

WARNER BOOKS

A Warner Communications Company

WARNER BOOKS EDITION

Copyright © MCMLXXVII Film Properties International N.V.
All rights reserved.

ISBN: 0-446-89329-3

Cover design by Sidney Ganis

Warner Books, Inc., 75 Rockefeller Plaza, New York, N.Y. 10019

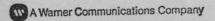 A Warner Communications Company

Printed in the United States of America

Not associated with Warner Press, Inc. of Anderson, Indiana

First Printing: August, 1977

10   9   8   7   6   5   4   3   2   1

For VERITY,
who knows why.

I shall tell you a great secret, my friend. Do not wait for the last judgment. It takes place every day.

ALBERT CAMUS

A WILLIAM FRIEDKIN FILM

SORCERER

Starring ROY SCHEIDER

BRUNO CREMER • FRANCISCO RABAL •
AMIDOU • RAMON BIERI •
Production Design JOHN BOX • Screenplay
WALON GREEN • Associate Producer BUD
SMITH • Original Music TANGERINE DREAM
• Based on the novel "The Wages of Fear" by
Georges Arnaud • Directed and Produced by WIL-
LIAM FRIEDKIN • A Paramount-Universal Re-
lease TECHNICOLOR®

1

Veracruz.

Sunday afternoon. The ancient central plaza was at its liveliest and noisiest. From the balcony of Room 32 in the old Hotel Colonial, you could see slender shafts of gold light filter through the laurel and palm trees, casting bright patterns on the surging masses of balloon vendors, trinket salesmen, families, couples, derelicts, prostitutes, and the *mariachi* and marimba bands that wandered through the sidewalk cafés. The lone occupant of Room 32 looked forward to the weekly spectacle: the warm, moving colors, the brassy, dissonant music, the aroma of *café con leche* mixed with the scent of heavily seasoned red snapper, stuffed crab, fried shrimp, broiled crayfish, and the first cool breezes of oncoming night. Across the street, on the south side of the plaza, the 242-year-old parish church, La Parroquia, seemed as cold and incongruous to the hap-

11

py mood as its flanking monstrosity to the east, the colonnaded Palacio de Gobierno, the state capitol. But the ritual of Sunday mass was over, the Day of Immaculate Conception wasn't celebrated until the following Wednesday, and, for the past week, the newspapers had told the sad story of what had been going on in domed structures like the Palacio all over Mexico—a drastic devaluation of the peso that signaled severe austerity programs for years to come.

Leaning against his balcony railing, the man smiled faintly, gazing across at those two enormously undistinguished buildings. In his early fifties, lean, of average height, he still retained in his posture vestiges of protracted military discipline, and the lift of the chin was still unconsciously arrogant, despite the faded, worn, and almost studied casualness of his clothes. The subject of history had been a passion from the time of his childhood in Geretsried, near the Isar, where his father had been a dairy farmer, and he had concentrated on history at the University of Munich, with emphasis on the separation of church and state. When he arrived in Veracruz from Haiti just five months before, one of the first luxuries he allowed himself was a visit to an island only a short distance offshore, where members of the Juan de

12

Grijalva expedition landed in 1518. They named it the Isle of Sacrifices, because of the bloodstained temples and horribly mutilated human remains. As in all previous civilizations, and those to emerge later, men had butchered each other in the name of a god or gods. The rationale and technical expertise alone had changed. From the time Cortez's fleet landed at Chalchiuhcueyacán in 1519, and renamed it Villa Rica de la Vera Cruz ("rich town of the true cross"), the place had been plagued by violence, primarily man-made, and the man in Room 32 understood the reasons and accepted them with the same historical perspective and clinical detachment that had made his military career successful, if unspectacular.

It was a simple, fortuitous circumstance of geography: because of its strategic and naturally protected location in the Gulf of Campeche, Veracruz had been Mexico's most important seaport for more than 450 years, and it still was. Military men wanted that seaport, and they still did. Pirates thrived on it for over a century. The city was invaded by the French in 1862, by the United States in 1847 and 1914, and it was threatened at other times by warships from Britain, France, Spain, and the U.S. Undoubtedly, it would be again.

Violence had been a way of life in Veracruz, and, to a lesser degree, it still was.
Despite its tropical atmosphere, it was never
developed as a vacation or tourist center.
Some tourists came, of course, and stayed at
relatively modern hotels like the Veracruz,
Mocambo, Emporio, and Ruiz Milán; you
would see them in the better restaurants and
sidewalk cafés, in the open-air trolley cars,
or in taxis headed for the Fort of San Juan
de Ulúa, just north of the city, with its noto-
rious dungeons that flooded at high tide. But,
by and large, these were the tourists who
had long since visited the glamour areas of
Mexico, the veteran travelers who had done
it all and wanted something different. They
found it in Veracruz, but not in historical
relics. They found it in the streets. They
found it in the unusually high percentage of
expatriates—predominately middle-aged and
older men—American, British, German and
French, in that order; ostensibly not writers
or artists, but obviously misfits of one kind
or another, strange men with unconventional
manners and habit patterns, few with visible
means of support. You'd see them in bars
just off the plaza, late at night, alone or in
very small groups; sitting in the lobbies of
small hotels, reading foreign newspapers;
standing outside the post office in the early

morning, waiting for the opening. They were too numerous to miss and too furtive to ignore. They were different. If you observed them for only a few days and nights, you couldn't help asking yourself: Who the hell are they? What are they doing in Veracruz? Why are they so frightened?

Frightened, that was the word. If there was any common denominator, that was it. Not frightened the way a junkie is, or a professional crook, or a psycho. Not frightened of losing dignity or identity. And, surprisingly, not frightened by the police. No, it was something else. You knew it almost intuitively when you watched their eyes in the plaza, the way they smoked, the way they sat in corners, the way they watched certain reflections in store windows. So the next question was: If you weren't afraid of traditional authority, of the law enforcement structure of a country like Mexico, where foreigners were regularly jailed for the slightest infraction, then what other authority could terrify you to the extent of living like a hunted animal? And why in Veracruz? Did the severe law enforcement here provide the kind of special protection needed by those men? Or were the officials here simply more corrupt than in other cities, providing the necessary entry visas and guaranteeing political asylum and police protection for those who could afford the initial and subsequent costs? Fascinating questions for seasoned tourists; excellent fuel for conversation when they got home.

The man in Room 32, who knew the answers to those questions only too well, was fascinated by a more simple question: down in the crowded, noisy plaza, a little Mexican girl, about six years old, was happily reeling in a huge dark-gray balloon in the shape of an octopus, its oval, helium-filled body looking bigger than she was, its eight long arms dancing above her as if in slow motion, reaching, twisting, stretching, its giant white eyes bulging, staring blindly, as if infuriated with its captor; why was the little girl laughing?

The man turned from the railing, went into the shade of the room to pour himself a drink. His eyes were drawn to the little voodoo doll on a shelf near the dresser, one of the few souvenirs he'd bought in Haiti. It was wooden, hand-carved and painted, a man in a black top hat, tuxedo, and white gloves; in the dim light, his face held a soft half-smile.

Before he reached the table with the single bottle of Johnnie Walker Red, he stopped abruptly, seeing a slender triangle of yellow

16

light on the bare wooden floor by the door. In the five months he'd been a resident of the hotel, the maids had startled him twice before in the late afternoon. They'd knocked softly before unlocking the door, but he'd been on the balcony both times and hadn't heard them enter. On each occasion, he'd reacted by shouting at them, then apologized, for they were merely delivering his routine order of *agua pura* for cocktails. He was about to mumble the usual *Buenas tardes*, when he caught a glimpse of the white shoes and dark trousers.

The silhouette in the open doorway was not imposing, only moderately tall and slender, wearing a narrow-brimmed hat. The man in Room 32 squinted, saw a split-second reflection of dark eyeglasses as the figure's right arm moved behind the back. Beyond the silhouette, the long, lighted hallway receded to an infinity of doors that seemed to blur now, then pulsate to the fast rhythms of loud, brassy, inharmonious *mariachi* and marimba music, a simultaneous combination of dreamlike, cacophonous tones, at unrest, needing completion.

The silhouette held a Mexican-manufactured Obregon .45 automatic. It was the best he could get in Mexico City, and he considered himself fortunate. When he squeezed the trigger, it gave the expected hard recoil, and he hit his target precisely where he'd intended, in the middle of the forehead, the bullet making a relatively small entry, but an exit approximately three times that size in the back of the skull.

2

JERUSALEM.

On Monday, December 6, the noon temperature was exactly seventy-three degrees as lunchtime crowds swarmed out of office buildings near the Damascus Gate, and the small sidewalk restaurants and falafel stands began filling with shirt-sleeved workers. Newspapers carried front-page stories about the first resolution to be submitted by Israel to the U.N. General Assembly in twenty-seven years of membership. Essentially a response to Arab peace moves, the resolution called for early reconvening of the Geneva Mideast conference, asking the assembly to urge Egypt, Israel, Jordan and Syria to meet "without delay" under the joint chairmanship of the United States and the Soviet Union. A memorandum accompanying the resolution said the conference "should be convened as originally constituted"—meaning without participation of the Palestine Liberation Organization. The PLO question had blocked resumption of the conference, which met for two days in December, 1972, and had not reconvened since.

Three young men, dressed in the sport shirts and jeans that were a kind of uniform for Israeli students, moved through the crowd toward a bus stop near the Bank of Israel, talking in Hebrew. Hakim, the oldest, in his late twenties, carried a small canvas duffel bag with a pair of track shoes tied to the handle; Sayid held a loose-leaf binder and two textbooks from a trade school; Kassem, the best-looking of the three, with relatively long, dark, curly hair framing a high forehead, carried a duffel bag almost identical to Hakim's, and practiced soccer kicks as they walked. They all wore yarmulkes.

"Heard it on the radio," Kassem said, laughing.

Hakim smiled, shifted the duffel bag to his other hand. "If it came from Golda herself, I wouldn't believe it."

"Heard it on Kol Israel," Kassem insisted. "It was just announced from Tel Aviv this morning. Israel's three hundred ritual circumcisers have formed a union to protect their mutual interests."

The third man, Sayid, didn't even crack a smile.

"I mean, shit," Kassem went on, skipping

into another kick, pushing back his hair. "If they didn't form a union, outsiders might undercut them."

Hakim had to laugh. "The Japs might enter the market."

"Might roll back the profits," Kassem said.

When they reached the bus stop in front of the bank building, Kassem and Hakim stepped back from the crowd, leaned against the white stone wall near the entrance, set down their duffel bags. A young girl was also leaning against the wall, reading a book.

Kassem looked the girl up and down, then asked Hakim for a cigarette.

"When you going to buy your own?" Hakim reached into his back pocket. "When you join the union?"

"Hell, no, I couldn't hack it in the union."

They both took a cigarette. As Hakim held the lighted match, his hand shook just perceptibly.

Kassem noticed, smiled. "You couldn't cut it, either. 'By the rivers of Babylon, there we sat down, yea, we wept, when we remembered Zion,' and our circumcision. Yea, it only hurt when we laughed."

They leaned back again and watched two young Israeli women soldiers who walked past slowly, caps slanted toward the left eyebrow, breasts bulging in tight khaki shirts with rolled-up sleeves, miniskirts that rose at least halfway up the thighs, sandals that looked almost fashionable. Their hair was down in back, which was permitted under the new regulations, along with very light lipstick and mascara, but they could wear only one ring, bracelet and necklace each, earrings that were no larger than the earlobe, and transparent nail varnish.

When the bus pulled in, disgorging passengers from the back door, boarding an equally large number in front, Kassem leaned down and pulled a small piece of wire from the zipper of his duffel bag. He took a final drag on the cigarette, then followed Hakim and Sayid into the bus, leaving the duffel bag behind. As the doors closed and the bus pulled away, he glanced at the bag.

It looked very small on the sidewalk near the entrance, up against the white stone wall. People drifted past in a steady stream of colors in the December sunlight, shoppers, students, executives, soldiers, orthodox Jews, secretaries, Arabs, old men with heavy loads on their backs, women with bundles on their heads. A few paused to check the schedule at the bus stop.

Exactly 120 seconds after Kassem had pulled the wire, the duffel bag exploded. It was a blast of tremendous force, heard over a circumference of ten square blocks, blowing a huge cavity in the wall, spraying stone and cement in its wake, killing three people instantly, injuring fourteen. An immediate shower of plate glass rained from the windows above, flashing through the heavy smoke, as cars and trucks skidded to stops, some careening into each other. People were screaming and running, a few toward the scene, most away from it.

Four blocks away, the muffled blast could be heard on the bus, and passengers turned, frowning, talking, straining to see through the rear window. The bus driver stopped the vehicle, because traffic in front of him had stopped. Everyone was looking back, but the traffic was too heavy to see anything except billows of thick gray-black smoke. Kassem, standing in the hot, crowded, noisy aisle, pushed back his hair, took out a pack of chewing gum, carefully unwrapped a stick, folded it in half, placed it in his mouth, dropped the wrappings on the floor. He chewed slowly for a while, then unwrapped another stick, folded it in half before taking it. Horns started blowing. People in cars and trucks were shouting at each other. The bus continued ahead in the heavy midday traffic.

Twenty-one minutes later, Kassem, Hakim and Sayid got off in a relatively quiet suburban neighborhood near David's Wall, walked slowly to their two-story, eight-unit apartment house. Inside, they climbed the short staircase quickly. Hakim knocked at the apartment door in a four-two-five combination. The door was opened and they were greeted by two men of approximately their age, also dressed like students. All five men began speaking in rapid Arabic.

Kassem crossed the dark living room to the front window and lifted a slat in the drawn blinds. The sunny, palm-lined street seemed deserted in both directions, except for parked cars. He continued to chew the gum slowly, pushed a lock of curly hair from his high forehead, then removed his yarmulke. Hakim threw his duffel bag and track shoes on the couch, grabbed an El Al flight bag from the coffee table, removed a nickel-plated Colt .45 automatic in a shoulder holster, and began putting it on over his head. Sayid opened his suitcase on the couch, withdrew a Walther 9mm Parabellum P-38, began looking for the clip.

The radio was on, a newscaster speaking calmly in Hebrew:

"Businesses in many towns in Israeli-held Arab territory closed their doors today to protest the levy of a new sales tax by the government. A military spokesman said, however, that in the occupied West Bank only two towns, Hebron and Halhoul, were affected by the strike. Students threw stones and burned tires in Nablus, thirty-five miles north of Jerusalem, but dispersed quickly, the spokesman said. The strike was total in the Gaza Strip. Although the eight percent value-added tax actually went into effect in Israel in July, it was postponed until December first in the occupied areas, after a general strike in the West Bank lasted several weeks."

Kassem continued to look out the window. "Was it on the news yet?"

"Yes," one of the new men said. He was tall and wore thin tortoise-shell glasses which he was constantly adjusting. "Just a short news bulletin."

"At least three dead, scores injured," the other one said, approaching Kassem. He was abnormally thin, looked almost emaciated.

"Change the station," Kassem told him. "See if you can find another—" He blinked, lifted the slot in the blinds higher to observe a middle-aged man walking slowly along the street from the direction of David's Wall. Although the man was dressed in civilian clothes, Kassem sensed something about him, about the casual way he walked. From the opposite direction, another man appeared, crossing the street, walking toward the apartment, glancing up at the window. Kassem stopped chewing his gum.

At that point, everything happened with the astonishing speed that only a meticulously planned and professionally executed military operation could hope to achieve. A brown flatback army truck swung around the corner, carrying at least a dozen members of the elite Border Police in combat fatigues and helmets, and skidded to a stop directly in front of the apartment. In an instinctive reaction, Kassem bolted for the door, ran out in the hallway, heard Hakim's voice shouting, followed instantly by the sound of glass breaking and two very loud gunshots. Shaking, panicky, thinking irrationally, Kassem sprinted for the stairs, heard glass shattering at the front door, turned and ran down the hall for the fire stairs.

Three members of the Border Police, led by a thin, wiry captain named Sassi, broke in the front door and scrambled up the short staircase, all carrying .45-caliber submachine guns. The tall young man with the tortoise-shell glasses ran out of the apartment door too fast for anyone to see that he was unarmed, and Captain Sassi fired immediately, hitting him in the face and neck. He screamed, ran blindly into the wall, bounded back, hit the floor flat on his back, bleeding from the eyes, mouth and neck, legs still moving. The captain quickly assumed a crouched position, entered the apartment firing, and Hakim was hit in the back by pure chance. He whirled away from the window, fired wildly, and the captain sprayed a volley that caught him in the chest, neck, eye and forehead. Another officer, crouched and firing from the doorway, hit the very skinny kid in the back and head as he tried to run behind the couch.

In the abrupt silence that followed, smoke drifted in layers and the smell of gunpowder was very strong. Captain Sassi stood up, cautiously, motioned for the officer in the doorway to stand. Sayid's voice could be heard from the little bedroom, speaking in Hebrew: "I surrender. I surrender."

By that time, about a dozen people were already out in the street, including tenants of the building, evacuated by other members of the Border Police. Within five minutes, two police cars arrived, then an ambulance, a police van, and several cars filled with army personnel. When people in neighboring houses and apartment buildings were confident that it was safe, they came over for a look. In less than fifteen minutes, a relatively large crowd had gathered on the sidewalk and spilled into the street, and the rumor was circulating that the police had just captured a number of Arab terrorists. Kassem was in the crowd, mingling, asking questions, chewing his gum. It was one of the safest places for him in the entire area.

Somebody yelled that a prisoner was being brought out, and people moved closer to the entrance. Two Border Police officers led Sayid down the stairs and through the front door, handcuffed, and the crowd immediately surged forward for a closer view. Men shouted insults and obscenities at him, and several people in front spat at him, but he was quickly surrounded by officers and ushered along toward the van. On the way, the crowd pushed still closer, and Kassem, realizing they were headed his way, tried to draw back, but couldn't. Seconds after Sayid was shoved into the van and seated, facing the rear doors, an officer on either side, he caught a glimpse of Kassem.

They stared at each other in silent communication, faces dripping with sweat, listening to the insults, until the doors were slammed.

3

The large and well-maintained *fin-de-siècle* houses along Avenue Foch were bathed in gold light Wednesday morning, December 8, giving the impression of a more favorable age, broken only by an occasional Peugeot or Citroen parked at the curb. From the window of his living room, Victor Manzon watched four children on their way to school, wearing smart navy-blue uniforms, but looking chilly in the forty-eight-degree temperature. Although he had already dressed to the point of shirt and trousers, his body was unmistakably hard and disciplined, looking more like that of a professional athlete than an investment banker. His face was lean and angular, too, not handsome, but not hard, and his hair was worn relatively long, the coloring difficult to detect. He was pensive that morning, his eyes lacked the usual life and humor, but

29

when he turned from the window and walked through the lavishly appointed living room, clearing his throat, he made an effort to change his mood. He entered the bedroom, went to the dresser, selected a pair of cuff links from a black leather stud box.

His wife Blanche was still in bed, reading the manuscript of a book, pencil in hand. In the lamplight, even without make-up, her face revealed the kind of mid-life beauty that characterizes certain French women, an elusive *joi de vivre* from within, extremely difficult to fake.

Victor adjusted his cuff links and walked toward his tie rack. As he passed the bed, his eye was drawn to a pile of edited manuscript pages on the floor. He picked them up. "What're you working on?"

"It should be our big nonfiction book for the year. If I ever get it edited."

He nodded, read the title page. " '*The Foreign Legion*, A Memoir, by Colonel Ettien Debray.' " He smiled, handed her the pages, crossed the room to his tie rack. "Action adventure, the glory of Colonial France. Another soldier-poet?"

"More philosopher than soldier." She put on rather severe reading glasses, leafed through the manuscript, frowned, began reading softly. " 'The cannons were trained on the village. Soon I would lower my hand

and the firing would begin. Through my field glasses, I could see a woman with a jar of water on her head, walking slowly towards her home, as she had done every day of her life. Within seconds, I would make a simple gesture that would remove her from the face of the earth. Whose gesture would remove me? When and how would it come?' "

Victor stopped at the edge of the bed, on his way to the bathroom. "Did he lower his hand?"

"Yes."

"Then he was just a soldier."

"No one is 'just' anything." She watched him enter the bathroom, then sat forward, seeing his reflection in the long mirror.

He began threading his tie through his collar, glanced down and saw the old tin Band-Aid box placed in an obvious position by the side of the sink. Blanche had bought it in New York ten years ago, during their round-the-world honeymoon trip, and could never seem to part with it. He smiled, opened the lid, and Blanche studied his face as he removed the gift, a gold Lucien Piccard wristwatch that had cost a full one-quarter of her annual salary. He turned it over and saw the inscription: IN THE TENTH YEAR OF FOREVER. Deeply moved, and aware now that Blanche was watching, he managed a poker face as he strapped it on his left wrist, then casually began tying his tie, taking his time, getting the knot just right, his face expressionless. The charade lasted until he took his suit coat from the wooden valet and unintentionally glanced at her in the mirror. Her expression was so utterly perplexed that he laughed out loud, tossed his coat on the valet, ran out and literally dived into bed, hugging and kissing her.

She laughed like a little girl, out of breath. "Do you like it? I never know! Is it perfect or just okay?"

"I adore it and I love you."

"Still?"

"Still and always."

"Happy anniversary, darling."

* * *

Victor Manzon believed what Ruskin said: "Great nations write their autobiographies in three manuscripts, the book of their deeds, the book of their words, and the book of their art. Not one of these books can be understood unless we read the two others, but of the three the only trustworthy one is the last." Virtually every time Victor arrived at the Paris Bourse, and walked up the white

marble steps, aware of the stately, colonnaded, Neo-Grecian façade, he was at least
subliminally reminded of Ruskin's statement.
He knew the appalling history of deeds
transacted in this stock exchange, he heard
and read on a daily basis the hypocritical
words of mutual respect and honorable in-
tention, and he had finally come to trust and
believe only in the façade. It alone maintained the appearance of dignity and
strength. What went on inside was often an
utterly ludicrous travesty played by actors
who neither understood nor really cared
about the underlying, frightening forces at
work: the stock market was, in fact, nothing
more or less than a mirror in a highly sophisticated telescope, reflecting the ostensible economic situation, like the light from
a distant star that took many years, often
many lifetimes, to reach us. Its actual condition in any given year was unknown in
time present. When a cataclysmic event was
taking place in the economic affairs of a
nation, an industry, a company, or an individual, the disaster was usually a *fait ac-
compli* long before it was in sight.

That morning, December 8, Victor was
keeping an appointment with Gustave Lefevre, chairman of the Paris Bourse, whose
office was as large, opulent and cold as the

man himself. Sitting behind a Louis XV desk, Lefevre looked every bit as grave as those former Bourse officials in the oil paintings that cluttered his walls. His friend Guillot, a former chairman, was seated at a side table with a third man, not introduced to Victor, who took notes of their conversation.

Lefevre launched into his role without the usual preliminaries. "We're not speaking about the levy of a fine for carelessness. We're speaking about *fraud*. A criminal act. The deliberate misrepresentation of collateral for the purpose of rampant speculation —fifteen million francs."

Victor nodded quickly. "The firm has already made arrangements to cover the deficit."

"For the full amount?"

"Yes."

Guillot frowned. "How?"

"A guarantee."

"What guarantee?"

"My father-in-law."

Lefevre glanced at his desk. "My position demands I turn over all information for immediate criminal prosecution."

"Let me ask," Victor said calmly, "if you couldn't see a way to give a twenty-four-hour reprieve to a firm that's over a hundred years old. You know the effect this will have on the Preville family."

Lefevre considered in silence for a while. "The fall of an important investment house in these times hurts everyone." He removed an envelope from his coat pocket, tossed it across the desk. "I received this yesterday at my home. I think the intent is obvious."

Victor took the envelope, sat back, opened it quickly. It contained a handwritten note on pale-gray watermarked stationery with the Preville family crest.

7 December 1976

M. Lefevre,

The long and amicable association which you have had with my family would of course be strengthened by any personal consideration that you might find possible to give us in these present complications.

I offer my personal guarantee that a tangible expression of our gratitude would be forthcoming.

Sincerely,
Pascal Preville

Visibly embarrassed, Victor read it a second time, placed it slowly back in the envelope, shook his head, spoke just above a whisper. "I can't believe this has happened."

"I know," Lefevre said softly. "Since this

is peripheral to the matter at hand, I'm going to forget I ever received it." In the pause, he watched Victor tuck the envelope into his coat pocket. "If I give you the time, and stop the criminal prosecution, there will still be fines and a suspension."

"I understand."

Lefevre checked his watch. "Before eleven tomorrow morning, if you present certified collateral to reestablish your credit, I'll hold back the criminal charges." He studied Victor's face. "I have your word this will happen?"

"Absolutely."

*   *   *

It was just past noon when Victor found a parking space in a courtyard off Place Vendôme, near the lovely old "Belle Epoque" building that was the principal office of Preville & Son. He sat in the car for a while, gazing out at the crowded, sunlit square that housed some of the most distinguished shops and offices in the city—Cartier, Schiaparelli, Van Cleef & Arpels, Caron, Elizabeth Arden, Boucheron—and overflowed into the Rue de la Paix. When Place Vendôme was designed by Jules Hardouin-Mansart in the late seventeenth century, the architectural proportions constituted a masterpiece of harmony, graceful and discreet, even to the equestrian statue of Louis XIV in the center, facing the Rue Saint-Honoré. But, as Victor had learned to accept philosophically, the insanity of the military mind had irreparably altered it, leaving behind a monument to violence and stupidity. The elegant statue of Louis XIV had been knocked down in the Revolution and finally replaced, in Napoleon's reign, by an ugly 145-foot vertical column, cast from the melted bronze of exactly 1,250 pieces of enemy artillery. That original monstrosity was toppled in 1871 by the Communards, at the urging of painter Gustave Courbet; following the violent Paris insurrection, Courbet was forced to pay for the column's reconstruction, a punishment that left him in financial and emotional bankruptcy. Victor couldn't suppress a grimace, looking at it in the noon sun. Again at 145 feet, hideously out of proportion with the surrounding architecture, its bronze weathered shades of green, the Vendôme Column was engraved with spiral bas-reliefs depicting the major events of the First Empire, and crowned by a statue of Napoleon draped in Roman garb. Victor always considered it the French phallic symbol *par excellence*; a haunting *coup de maître* of military megalomania.

Ironically, the column was a favorite of Baron Preville, his father-in-law, who had distinguished himself in both world wars, who had been elected to the Legion of Honor, who was a devotee of Napoleon, and who, in the final analysis, was the only one with the financial resources to bail him out of criminal prosecution. Despite what Victor had told Lefevre that morning, the Baron hadn't guaranteed anything; Pascal Preville, his son, hadn't even kept him up-to-date on exactly how serious the situation had become. Victor couldn't bring himself to tell his wife, much less ask her to plead the case to her father. But Pascal, her brother, was another matter. Pascal was just as guilty as he was, and had just as much to lose. If the Baron refused, they would certainly be prosecuted, and, considering the amount of money involved, they would very probably wind up in prison. The Baron wouldn't let that happen. But Pascal would have to get to him fast.

When Victor entered the office, Pascal was standing near the fireplace, a young man with somewhat weak but aristocratic good looks. Victor decided to take a firm stand immediately, and read Pascal's letter to Lefevre out loud, angrily, hoping to embarrass him.

Finishing in disgust, he flung the letter at Pascal's feet. "I've committed everything I own and every penny I have to saving this firm, and your contribution is *this*. Thanks to your naïve gesture, we could be in jail this *minute*. By some miracle, he gave us twenty-four hours. Our *only* chance is to call your father."

Pascal hesitated, went to the window. "He refused me before."

"Now it's *different*. Now we face *jail*. The Baron would never suffer that disgrace. For his son-in-law, maybe; but not for *you*, his male heir. *Call* him!"

"He's shooting at Fontainebleau. I can't reach him before one o'clock."

"You must reach him today. Make him understand there's no other *choice*."

❋ ❋ ❋

Fishing was the chief occupation in Boulogne-sur-Mer when the Romans sailed from that squalid little port on the English Channel to conquer Britain in 43 A.D. It was the chief livelihood when that medieval countship became part of France in 1477, and most men fished for a living in Boulogne-sur-Mer when Napoleon gathered his forces there in 1804, intending to invade England.

They fished for a living there during World War I, when it was a principal port of the British Expeditionary Force. They fished for a living throughout World War II, when the place was evacuated by the British in the spring of 1940, and when it was recaptured by the Canadians in the autumn of 1944. They fished for a living in the dark morning hours of December 8, 1976, sold the best of their lobsters to representatives of the Rungis Wholesale Market, who rushed them by refrigerated truck to the stark, new, antiseptic-looking market, "the belly of Paris," by 5 a.m., and the very best of the lot were purchased at dawn by the highly selective buyer of the Pre-Catalan restaurant. Early that afternoon, the lobsters served to Victor and Blanche Manzon, and their friend Lydia Lamettrie, looked and tasted about the same as they had to the fishermen of Boulogne-sur-Mer two centuries past. The price and embellishments alone had changed.

Changed to the extent that only the wealthy lunched and dined at the Pre-Catalan now, and with the style and delight that only the affluent French seemed able to show. Lydia had been invited to the anniversary luncheon because she was Blanche's closest friend, and Victor was content to let the two women carry the conversation, absorbed in thoughts of his own. After two

40

glasses of the superb Château d'Yquem, his mood seemed to brighten, but he remained silent.

Blanche wore a new pink Courrèges dress, and a gold talisman pendant that she fingered frequently as she talked. "But the diversity of dialectic alone would keep them apart. A true alliance of socialists and communists is theoretically impossible."

Lydia, in a Saint Laurent whipcord skirt and a cashmere top, glanced down and away, chewing, elegant features dominated by dark brown eyes. "But not politically. First they agreed to unite to form a bloc. Then they spent the rest of the conference trying to upstage each other." She touched the napkin to her lips. "The lobster is excellent. In Mexico, they kept telling us about the lobster in Veracruz, so we finally went there, and they were disgusting."

"It's the water," Blanche told her. "Too warm. They must have cold. Right, darling?"

Victor nodded.

"Victor's father was a fisherman. He knows everything about seafood."

A waiter approached the table, leaned to Victor's side, spoke quietly. "Excuse me, Monsieur Manzon; a gentleman outside to see you."

Victor seemed slightly surprised, but recovered quickly, dabbed the napkin to his lips as he stood up.

"What is it, darling?"

He pushed in his chair. "Nothing. I have to sign a paper. Be right back."

As Victor reached the small lobby, Pascal was standing by the front door, hands in his pockets, looking extremely worried. Victor escorted him outside.

Pascal's voice shook. "He said *we* took the risk, *we* must bear the consequences. What*ever* they are."

Victor nodded, squinted in the cold sunlight, walked Pascal toward the parking area. Beyond the rows of cars, the enormous trees of the Bois de Boulogne still held most of their leaves, faded from the bright colors of autumn, fragile and proud in dying. Now only a reminder of the once-gigantic Rouvre Forest, around which Henri II constructed a wall from Auteuil to Neuilly, the Bois de Boulogne had become more of a park than a forest, and very popular in the summer months, but Victor always lamented the way it had been ravaged—by military men, of course, who cared nothing about the environment, or ecology, or trees that had taken centuries to grow. Oh, he knew about the hundreds of duels that took place in that forest prior to the Revolution, but that was entirely different: those men—and a few women—merely butchered each other by mutual consent; they didn't destroy or mutilate masses of people or large chunks of landscape. Yet, for ten solid years, 1789-1799, Revolutionary troops had used the Bois as a source of firewood. And the *coup de grace* occurred in 1815, in the aftermath of Waterloo: when British troops finally broke up their campsites, not a single, solitary oak tree was still standing. The Nazis camped here too, of course, but by that time the real forest was only a memory.

Walking toward the parking area, the two men were aware of the strong smell of decaying leaves. Their footsteps made soft, slow crunching sounds on the gravel. But Pascal was breathing rapidly.

"Calm down," Victor told him. "You've got to speak to him again."

"Yes." He took several deep breaths. "Yes, I'll drive to Fontainebleau. I'll do it right now, this afternoon."

Victor placed his hand on the man's shoulder. "I know this is hard for you, but I'm positive you can convince him. When he understands what it means to the family, he'll agree."

The top of Pascal's dark Porsche Targa held soft reflections of the trees. They stood by it for a moment, looking at the pale brown façade of the Pre-Catalan. The old restaurant's many windows sparkled, and couples were clearly visible, enjoying lunch. Pascal got in the car, closed the door, opened the window, then sat motionless, staring straight ahead.

He gripped the steering wheel very hard, shook his head quickly, decisively. "I can't do it. What if he refuses me to my face?"

"He won't. He'll act to save the firm. After you speak to him, this will all be over."

Victor started to say something else, decided against it, turned and walked back to the restaurant, listening to his footsteps on the gravel, waiting for Pascal to start the engine. When he reached the front steps, he heard the muffled sound of a gunshot. He ran back to the car. The large rear window of the Porsche was shattered and streaked red. As he came around to the side, he saw Pascal's head tilted back against the seat. He had shot himself in the mouth.

Victor turned away quickly, started walking, stopped. For a few seconds, he thought he was going to vomit. He took a deep breath, shoved his hands in his pockets, kept his head averted. Wind brought the sharp smell of decaying leaves. Without looking at the car again, he walked slowly back to the restaurant. His body began shaking.

He crossed the lobby and paused in an alcove leading to the dining room, waiting for his eyes to adjust. The room seemed bright yellow and slightly blurred. People at the tables were laughing and talking; silverware clinked softly. When the blurring stopped, he focused on Blanche and Lydia, engaged in a lively conversation. The whole room seemed unreal, a fragment from a dream. He started forward, but a strange force prevented him from entering that dining room. Something inside him would simply not allow him to walk to the table, reveal to Blanche that her brother had just killed himself, that her family was in disgrace, and that he faced prison. The room seemed unreal. Feeling dazed, he walked back to the lobby.

The headwaiter, studying his reservations book, looked up as Victor approached. "Monsieur Manzon?"

Victor took out his wallet, removed a crisp ten-franc note, handed it to him, cleared his throat softly to test his voice. "Please tell Madam that I had to leave on business."

"Of course, Monsieur. Thank you." The man slipped the note in his pocket, walked toward the dining room.

Gathering himself, Victor went to the front door, down the steps, and squinted in the bright light. From the moment he smelled the trees, he began shaking again, started to perspire. Breathing rapidly, he forced himself to look at the Porsche in the parking area. It became a blur in the sharp glare, its dark lines wavering, melting upward. He glanced at the watch his wife had given him only that morning, began to walk quickly, jogged, then ran. Toward the road at the edge of the Bois de Boulogne.

4

That screening room in Dodge Hall had the oldest furniture in the university, broken-down chairs and sofas of every description, and a total seating capacity of maybe sixty, if you pushed it, but there were about ninety students in the class. When my brother arrived that night, December 9, big film can under his arm, the room was jammed, hot and noisy, windows half open, smoke drifting to the high, beamed ceiling, and I remember how he maneuvered his way past the crowd by the door, then stepped carefully over and around the kids sitting on the floor, packed tightly all the way up to the long movie screen. He stood at the wooden lectern to the right of the screen, a relatively short, chunky guy, unruly hair and beard, and pushed at the nosepiece of his glasses, as he always did, looking at his lecture notes. When he lit his first cigar, I noticed that he

47

was wearing two watches, one on each wrist, and a crazy Indian pendant over his red T-shirt, so I knew he was in a happy mood.

He began: "The film you're about to see . . ." and, almost immediately, all talking in the room stopped. That was a trick he used. "The film you're about to see," he went on, softer this time, "is actually a screen test, a rather lengthy one, that I made several years ago in an attempt to raise about a hundred and sixty thousand dollars for a ninety-minute television documentary about a prostitute in New York. It's called *Nicole*. We didn't get the money, the backers were too scared. They had a shit hemorrhage when they saw the screen test. I still think it'd make a good film, about a brilliant, talented woman. As far as I know, nobody's ever done a documentary about the inside of a whorehouse, the inside workings. It should be done."

He opened his mouth then, as if yawning, as he always did when he was straining for a word or an idea. "Will you tell me something? On the list of this season's news-hour films, where's a *personal* documentary? Where's the film about a guy who went abroad to protest and dodge the draft, and might come back now, if Jimmy Carter keeps his campaign promise next month? Where's the film about that lonely girl searching for a man through an endless procession of singles weekends? Where's the film about a man dying from lung cancer? These films are not on any list, not one of them. They're not even in the planning stages. In Eugene O'Neill's *The Iceman Cometh*, the derelict says, 'Hickey, they've taken the life out of the booze.' *I* tell you, they've taken the life out of the *film*. Why?"

I was sitting in the last row, next to the projection booth, and enjoying it. I never went to college, much less Columbia, but Kevin let me sit in on the same documentary film course three years before, when I was on a belated education kick. Kevin was the only brain our family ever had, as far as I know. He went to the same schools in Queens that my sister and I went to, but he was the only one who really made a success of himself. He was something else. Word-of-mouth made his courses among the most popular at Columbia. When he got emotional about something during a lecture, or even when he was showing a film, he'd use the wildest language you ever heard in a classroom. I really admired the guy. He was sort of weird by academic standards. He didn't really give a shit what the administration thought about him or his ideas. It wasn't his full-time job, anyway. As an associate professor of film, he taught only a couple of courses a term, nights. He earned his real bread as a staff producer at CBS News.

"Why?" he repeated, like always, glancing around the room, flicking his cigar ash on the floor.

"Simple," a girl's voice said softly. "The executives in charge of programming are assholes."

"That may be true," he told her, "but that's a value judgment, not an answer to the question."

"They target the lowest common denominator," she said.

He chewed the cigar, thought about it. "Yeah, obviously, that's part of the problem. But I think a bigger part is that the people in charge of news at the networks, the presidents and vice-presidents of the news divisions, came out of the tradition of reportage. Many worked for newspapers or magazines or radio before television. They're word people. They're newsmen. They pride themselves on being reporters. They're in their fifties and not hip to the new film. But beyond all this, there seems to be a deeper reason why the personal documentary is notable chiefly for its absence. I think the reason is that we live in an increasingly uptight society. I think we're afraid of honest emotion. I think we dig all those facts and figures because they're so very remote. We can be detached. I think we're afraid of tenderness, afraid of anger, afraid of laying our guts on the table. I think we feel we have to keep the lid on very tight, because, if we don't, our kids are going to turn on, our blacks are going to kill, our poor are going to bust right into our living rooms and rip us off, and the whole mess is going to come unglued. I think all that fear exists. And we'd rather keep it nice and cerebral."

He paused then, took a puff on the cigar, reached up to scratch the back of his head, and I remember there was a hole in the armpit of his T-shirt. "As for me, I'd like a little less information and a lot more feeling. I think we know enough facts. What we don't know is how to feel. I think the goal of the filmmaker should be to make us more feeling, more human. We should try more to be novelists and poets of film, rather than such damn good reporters. I want to make people laugh and cry, and feel love and hate and pleasure and pain. I want to approach documentary with all the skill and sensibility that Fellini and Bergman and Godard bring to fiction films. But, at the networks, it's business as usual. They're working on next year's lists: a film on the legal profession, on Japan, on the affluent black, on tax-exempt foundations, and so on."

It went like that for about half an hour,

and, as usual, he made it extremely personal. That's one of the things that turned the kids on to him. He didn't hide behind the scholarly approach, the aloof bullshit that sounds so knowing and imposing it puts you to sleep. He took the responsibility for everything he said. And he'd listen to your side of it, if you wanted to say something. Anyway, when he was finished with the opening remarks, he stuck the big cigar (his second) in his mouth, picked up his film can and notes, made his way back through the kids to the projection booth, and motioned for me to follow him.

As I went into the booth, he was helping the young student projectionist to thread the film.

"A screen test about a *whore*house?" I said.

He laughed softly, cigar in his teeth. "Scandalous."

"Never saw that one."

"Wasn't made when you took the course, Jackie. You finish that book yet?"

I nodded, smiled. He'd made me read a book about cryonic suspension. You know, freezing people. He was really a pisser.

"See what I mean?" he asked.

"Good stuff for a documentary."

"You don't know the half of it." He stepped back, watched the projectionist run the film to the leader numbers, then removed his cigar and pointed to the door. "Tell them to hit the lights out there, huh?"

I opened the heavy door, shouted "Lights!" over the noise. Most of the talking stopped as the room went dark. When I closed the door, it took a while for my eyes to adjust. Then I saw the red tip of his cigar near the projector. I watched the film through the window in the door. The big numbers flashed backwards and the slateboard appeared, slightly out of focus. The projectionist sharpened it immediately, and then we saw a close-up of an attractive, dark-haired woman, probably the hooker, talking with someone off-camera. We couldn't hear the sound track in the booth. It was very quiet, except for the hum of the projector.

"Beautiful," Kevin said. "That's a classy, foxy lady."

"Where'd you shoot it?" I asked.

"Her apartment. Penthouse on East Sixty-fourth."

"She still in business?"

"Does the Pope shit in the forest? You couldn't afford it, anyway. Your week's salary wouldn't even buy a quickie from the maid. In the broom closet. On New Year's Eve. What's happening with Teamsters Local Eighty-four?"

"We're still out. They're still talking."

The tip of the cigar glowed as he walked toward me. "How you fixed for bread?"

"Getting by. That's about all."

"How long you been out now—seven weeks?"

"Eight weeks tomorrow."

He leaned against the door to my left, and I could see his profile in the changing light from the window. "Jackie, do yourself a favor, huh? Don't do anything foolish."

"What the hell you wearing two watches for?"

He thought about it. "Because I like them."

We laughed, glanced at each other. He took a final puff on the cigar, dropped it on the floor, stepped on it. It smelled awful.

"You're really a slob," I said softly. "You know that, don't you?"

He laughed, coughed, reached into the front pocket of his jeans. "A bright slob. A very, very bright slob. What can I tell you?" He took my right hand, pushed a small wad of bills into it.

"Oh, no, Kevin. No way."

"Bullshit. They won't have that thing settled by Christmas. Christmas is coming, for Christ's sake. What you going to do about Christmas presents? It's a loan, it's not a gift. I expect every nickel of it back when you go back to work."

I shoved it in his pocket. Hard. "I appreciate it, but I can't take it. I just can't."

He nodded, leaned back against the door. "Okay, okay. I know better than to argue with you. Just do yourself a big favor."

"Don't sweat it. I got enough to last."

"That's what you said last time."

"I didn't know we'd be out that long."

He took a cigar out of his back pocket, removed it from the metal cylinder. "You're forty-three years old, Jackie. Do yourself a favor, huh? Look at the percentages of getting caught." He smelled the cigar, bit off the end, spat it on the floor.

*　*　*

We'd already had it planned in detail for the following Sunday, December 12, at Our Lady of the Snow church in Elizabeth, New Jersey. It was based on reliable inside information. All the Catholic churches in East Jersey actually pooled their Sunday collections, and the money was held for a period of six months in a number of safe deposit boxes at a bank in Newark. In theory, the ranking clergy then assumed the responsibility of dividing up the money among all the churches, based on individual needs. If that theory had been followed in practice, all the churches in the low-income areas would have benefited greatly, but those churches and schools were as dirt-poor in the 1970s as they were in the 1930s. If you had any connection with organized crime, you knew why. And you weren't especially shocked, if you knew East Jersey. Every six months, four priests from the biggest parishes would have the pool money delivered by armored car to Our Lady of the Snow church, and they'd divide it up fairly, after they skimmed it good. Don't get me wrong, we had absolutely no altruistic motives when we pulled the heist. We just needed the money. But, the way I figured it, they were worse crooks than us.

Anyway, on that particular Sunday, it was a clear and cool afternoon in Elizabeth, temperature about forty-five or so, and we were parked just down the street from the Shell station, which was across the street from the church. At 2:15, there were around fifty people out on the front lawn of the church, because a wedding was scheduled for 2:30. That was also the time the armored car was scheduled to pull into the parking lot behind the church, and not by coincidence; the good fathers reasoned that there was always safety in numbers. What they didn't understand was that a big wedding crowd also made dynamite camouflage for legitimate crooks.

Irish, rather than Italian. I mean, the good Lord takes care of his own.

We used my car, but with different plates, a yellow, four-door 1972 Chevy that I'd bought from my brother-in-law the previous spring. Donnelly was in the seat next to me, and Murray and Boyle were in back. We were dressed in our best shanty-Irish wedding suits, and I wore a topcoat that had two sets of handcuffs in each of the inside breast pockets. Donnelly had made me go to four of those dipshit S-and-M stores and buy only one pair of cuffs in each store. I thought that was carrying caution to an extreme, but Donnelly had done time once for being careless, so he worked things out to the smallest detail. He was what we called the leadoff man, and he was also the chopper. I didn't even carry a gun; I was just the wheel man. We were all about the same age, except Murray, who was in his thirties, I think. Murray was swag man, and so was Boyle. We needed two, because there was a hell of a lot of cash to carry, and we couldn't use bags or anything like that. Murray and Boyle had special vests with rows of deep pockets. We made a good group. We'd all known each other for years, but we'd only pulled one other job together, when we had the real long strike. We were in the same union local up in Queens.

I remember feeling more nervous the longer we waited, and I knew Donnelly was jumpy, too, because he couldn't seem to stop talking. He just kept on and on, you couldn't shut the guy up.

"You see the paper this morning?" he asked nobody in particular. "They got a Santa Claus rumble brewing. About control of the jingle-bell turf around Manhattan. You see that? Up to Fifth Avenue, Rockefeller Center, all like that. The regular Santas, the guys that stand by the little chimneys and ring the bells—right?—they're sponsored by an outfit called the Volunteers of America. So now they got competition. First time. You believe this? That religious sect, what do they call them?"

"Hare Krishna," I said.

"Yeah, that's them, the Hare Krishnas. Right? Them freaky-looking kids with the shaved heads and long robes and that. So now they're wearing Santa Claus suits and beards, the whole thing. They're out in the streets, prime locations at Fifth, Grand Central, the Garden, trying to muscle in on the regular Santas."

"Don't they have a union?" Boyle asked.

Donnelly didn't turn around, didn't even stop longer than a smirk. "These freaks, these ballbreakers, not only do they ask people for donations, they grab them by the *arm* and follow them down the *block*. You believe this? Hassling the *shit* out of them. So now the regular Santas, as of yesterday, they've had it. I mean, the freaks are giving them a bad name, right? Plus the fact they're losing donations like crazy. So now they're—"

He saw the signal. We all saw it. The Shell sign on the pole at the gas station began to revolve slowly. The lookout we had there (who only pumped gas on weekends, moonlighting from his regular job) had seen the armored car arrive at the back parking lot.

I checked my watch—they were two minutes early—pulled away from the curb, drove slowly toward the gas station, then took a left and passed the church. We could see the two Brinks guards walking to the back door in the bright sunlight, each holding a pistol down at his right side and carrying a large white sack. I slowed to let another car enter the parking lot ahead of me, followed him in, found an empty space. We all got out, straightening our ties and coats, smoothing our hair, and walked around to the front. We could see our breath in the air.

There seemed to be a lot of teenagers in the crowd out front, which unnerved me a little, but then I noticed enough people of our own age, and older; they were just standing in separate groups from the kids. We moved toward an older-looking group, stopped, took out cigarettes, began shooting the breeze. Several cars pulled up to the curb right in front, an area marked off for members of the wedding party. I remember one of them was a mid-sixties Buick, in reasonably good shape, decorated with bunting, streamers, and with tin cans tied to the rear bumper. Four young men got out, dressed in the latest-style formal wear.

We decided to split up at that point, very casually, and moved as individuals through the crowd, smiling, nodding, trying to blend in. I noticed the armored car driving away. After the three men in the wedding party entered the church, we heard the organ music start, the usual warm-up to the wedding march, and the crowd began moving inside quickly. There was a sign over the entrance: *Friday Night Bingo*. I caught a glimpse of the bride-to-be, standing just inside the door, a very pretty kid of about seventeen, trying to smile at everybody, but looking scared as hell. I went in, stood in back.

When the wedding march started, the organizing relatives somehow managed to get everyone into a formal lineup, and, moments before the bride and groom started down the aisle, I followed Donnelly, Boyle and Murray, who slipped out a side door and walked down a cement staircase. When I caught up to them, they were standing in the corridor that led to the basement doorway. Simultaneously, we put on our dark glasses and pulled out our knit caps. When Donnelly put his cap on, he looked so God damn ludicrous I almost laughed. I can see him now, stepping to the door, pausing with his hand on the knob. Our informant swore up and down that the door would be open, but I remember thinking: *What if it's not?* There we'd be, standing there in our dark glasses and dumb knit caps, looking at each other, not knowing whether to shit or go blind. In the pause, we heard the rhythmic clicking of an adding machine from inside.

He turned the knob, opened the door, walked in nonchalant as you please, no gun, nothing. "All right, all you humps, get up against the wall."

I recall it was a small room, brightly lighted, windowless, and the four priests counting money at the table looked up at us with expressions like they'd just been caught jerking off. Murray closed the door. Chairs scraped loudly as the priests stood. Boyle and I flanked Donnelly, slightly behind, out of any possible line of fire. There was more cash on that table than I think I'd ever seen in one place at one time. We all went to work fast. I pulled out the first pair of handcuffs, grabbed the nearest priest by the arm, shoved him toward a steampipe that ran from floor to ceiling. Boyle and Murray went to the table, opened their coats, began stuffing the stacks of bills in their special vests. I cuffed the first priest's hands around the steampipe, grabbed another; he pulled back and I had to yank him with both hands.

The oldest priest, a heavyset Italian with almost pure white hair, was really fuming. "You know whose parish this is?"

"Shut up," Murray told him.

He glared at Murray, turned and walked quickly toward a door marked *Rectory*. Donnelly pulled his .38 with the four-inch silencer, shot the priest in the left thigh. It sounded louder than I expected. The old guy fell hard against the door, went down slowly, trying to hang on to the paneling.

Donnelly spoke quietly. "Crawl from now on, you fat zip."

"You're dead," the old man said, voice shaking. He turned on the floor, holding his thigh. "You're all dead."

Donnelly nodded, glanced at the two priests already cuffed around the pipe. He kept his voice incredibly calm. "We're either going to do this with your cooperation, or we're going to blow you away. It's up to you."

Murray and Boyle continued stuffing the cash in their vests. As I finished slapping

cuffs on the third priest, Donnelly went over
and gave the old one a swift kick in the ass.
The guy made a deep sound in his throat,
dragged himself toward the steampipe.
When I put the cuffs on him, I went easy.

By that time, Boyle and Murray had filled
all the pockets in their vests. There was still
some cash left on the table, but not much.
Boyle punched the total button on the adding machine; it whirred, clicked, the tape
jumped up a little, and he tore it off. We all
buttoned our coats and went to the door.
As the others were going out, I glanced
back. The whole thing looked weird. Thin
layers of smoke hanging near the table, and
beyond, in the corner, three priests standing
close together, hands around the steampipe,
and the old one sitting on the floor, all scowl-
ing at me, like a group of strange, suspicious
primates in the monkey house of a zoo. In
the silence, I heard faint organ music, the
happy kind they play at the end of weddings.

Outside, the music seemed louder. I
closed the door, took off the knit cap and
dark glasses, and the sunlight hurt my eyes.
Donnelly, Murray and Boyle were already
walking toward my car, one by one, leisure-
ly. Although I think the wedding ceremony
was over, nobody was in the parking lot yet,
and I knew they'd probably hang around out

front for some time, taking pictures and all
that, before leaving for the reception.

We took our time getting in the car. I
drove slowly out of the lot, headed in the
opposite direction from the way we came.
When we were a couple of blocks away, we
all began laughing softly.

"What's the total on the tape?" I asked
Boyle.

"Sixty-seven thousand dollars. And they
were still *counting*."

"Damned incredible," Donnelly said. As
he turned to look in back, I could smell the
smoke on his coat.

Murray's voice was unnaturally high.
"This is the entire collections from every
church in East Jersey from the last six
months. You know what this represents—
year after year, recession, depression, what-
ever—you know what these animals are cutting up?"

Donnelly nudged me. "Maybe they'll give
us a medal for this, Jackie."

"Who?"

"I don't know—the *Jews!*"

We all laughed, and I unconsciously
picked up some speed, feeling terrific relief
from all the tension. There was hardly any
traffic in either direction.

Donnelly leaned toward me, looked at the
speedometer. "Don't get us glommed."

"No way."

He smiled, shook his head. "The gas gauge says 'E.' What's that mean?"

"Exciting," I told him.

I'd figured out the best route back to Queens far in advance. The idea was to avoid the major highways until we got to a section of the Jersey Turnpike extension up above Newark Airport, take the Holland Tunnel into Manhattan, Canal Street down to Foley Square, Orchard up to Delancey, cross the Williamsburg Bridge, then pick up the Brooklyn-Queens Expressway all the way home to Jackson Heights.

So we were avoiding traffic, headed north on a two-lane street in an industrial section when it happened. I remember the back of a large truck lurched out from a driveway to my right. He backed out of there so God damn fast I must've acted on pure instinct, swerving left into the opposite lane, but he hit us almost broadside and with tremendous impact. Even with my seat belt on, my body was whipped to the right and forward like a rag doll and I felt my nose and forehead smash into the rear-view mirror. There was the sickening sensation of skidding sideways across the street, tires burning and squealing, then we slammed into some kind of pole and stopped dead.

All I remember about those first few seconds was the steady loud drone of the open-door warning buzzer, like my electric alarm clock, like waking up from a dream. Then a fast gurgling of water just before a fire hydrant blew, right by the left front fender, spouting a thick jet of water high in the air. It sounded like heavy rain on the roof, and the windshield blurred and took colors. The bridge of my nose started to hurt badly. When I touched it and looked at the blood on my fingers, I felt suddenly dizzy. Above the buzz, above the rain, the sound of someone crying softly, breathlessly, like a child. I looked to my right. Donnelly was jammed forward into a distorted position. His face was high up on the dash and the top of his head was locked in the shattered windshield. His left arm hung limply; blood ran from his fingers to the floor. He was trying to say something, but his mouth was pressed against the dash.

I tried to get away from him, but I couldn't. My arms and legs were moving in slow-motion, like swimming underwater. I tried to scream, but I couldn't hear my voice, only the buzz, the heavy rain, the crying. My hand went to my waist, clawing, and I felt the seat belt. I pushed the button and the belt snapped away and then I was fall-ing. I was on my back on the sidewalk, cold water pouring down on me. I scrambled up, moved away, saw an elderly man looking through the open back door. Boyle was sitting upright in there behind a thin curtain of water, eyes half open, bleeding heavily from the ears and nose.

The elderly man glanced at me. "That guy's gone."

A uniformed guard of some kind ran up to us, out of breath.

"That guy's gone," the man repeated.

A car screeched to a stop and another went by without even slowing down. The bridge of my nose began to throb. I touched it. Again, when I saw my own blood, I felt dizzy. I leaned against the pole. Murray was flat on his back in the street near the curb. He was moving a little, twisting; his coat was open, his vest was ripped, and there were loose bills on his chest, some sliding down. When I saw that, I knew I had to get out of there fast. It's funny how your mind works when you're in shock: I saw the money on Murray and suddenly realized that I didn't have any.

Several other cars came to a stop and people started running toward us. I remember going to my car, still dizzy, leaning in, unbuttoning Boyle's coat. My hands were shaking. I felt warm blood on my hands, yanked them back.

"No, you can't move him," the elderly man

told me. "You just got to leave him till the cops get here. He's gone."

One thing I'll have to say for the Jersey cops, they got there fast. The first squad car arrived no more than three or four minutes after the accident. At least, it seemed that way. They roared in with the siren screaming, jumped out, and the first person they reached was Murray. He wasn't moving any more. He looked dead. Loose bills were all over his chest, like a doll losing its stuffing.

One cop knelt down beside him. "Holy shit! Hey, Mickey!"

I remember wiping my nose on my sleeve, holding my nostrils, and walking back into the little crowd of motorists standing around. And, for some reason, I recall their faces vividly. Not one of them was looking at me. All, without exception, were staring at the dead.

* * *

That evening, the late edition of the *New York Post* had the whole story spread across page three, including a photograph of Murray in the street, and a very formal shot of the old Italian priest, taken years before. If Donnelly knew who that priest actually was, he'd also known enough to keep it a secret. My guess is that he simply didn't know. If

I'd known, I wouldn't have even considered going on the job, no matter how much money was involved. According to the *Post*, that old priest was Father Antonio Ricci, who happened to be the older brother of Carlo Ricci. If you don't live in New York, you might not know about Carlo Ricci. I knew his reputation from the time I was in grade school. He was the *capo* of one of the five so-called Mafia families in New York, but that's not all he was.

Before Frank Pescara died of a heart attack in October, 1976, at the age of seventy-four, he was the most powerful organized crime figure in the country, exerting the major influence—very quietly—over all five New York families, whose membership estimates ranged from 2,500 to 3,000 men, or about one-third of the national total. There are nineteen other families scattered around the country. New York has more families simply because it offers more for the taking. Of course, New York hadn't had an official, all-powerful *capo di tutti capo* since the five-family structure was set up in 1931, but there was always one man who had the strongest influence, because of several factors—age, experience, line of descent from the original hierarchy—and Frank Pescara had been that man for more than a decade, until last October. When he died, a new era in organized crime began, and it will undoubtedly be a more violent one than the decade presided over by the soft-spoken Pescara. Because the man who replaced him was Carlo Ricci.

Before Pescara officially banned narcotics as a source of Mafia revenue, Ricci's family found the profits far too tantalizing, and he'd been caught and convicted in 1961 on the extremely effective federal narcotics conspiracy laws. He'd served fourteen years in a federal prison, was released about a year before Pescara's death, and the word from the street was that he had taken over almost immediately. His long-range goal was to consolidate the five families into one. That had been tried before, many times, and always ended in bloodshed, because, with more than forty years of history behind each New York family, old alliances were not easily overcome.

Anyway, when I read in the *P*_____ we'd wounded Carlo Ricci's brother, I knew I was in big trouble—trouble so serious that I probably wouldn't beat it. I was the only one of the four of us who got out alive, and, although the press didn't have my name, I knew God damn well that Carlo Ricci would have it from the street in a matter of hours. He'd want me dead. It was as simple as that. I was a dead man if I didn't manage to get out of the country—not the city, the country

—immediately. Which was next to impossible. I had exactly $2,155 stashed in my apartment, which I grabbed, packed and ran with as soon as I read the *Post*. I checked into a third-rate hotel on Northern Boulevard out in Flushing, Queens, near Shea Stadium, then tried desperately to get my head together. I couldn't ask Kevin or my sister for help, because I knew Ricci's people would be watching them from the word go. I didn't even risk a call to them. Both my parents were dead, but I wouldn't have gone to them in any case. For the past few years, whenever I needed help, I'd leaned on Donnelly. I remember sitting on the bed in that hotel room, blinds drawn, door locked and chained, and writing down names of people I'd known, people who'd been friends at one time or another in my life, people from high school, from the neighborhood, from the union, from all the jobs I'd had, people who might possibly help me, people I could trust. The list wasn't very long. And, when I'd finished crossing the names out, being as realistic as I'd ever been in my life, it was down to one guy: Vinnie Reggio.

I'd kind of lost track of him over the years, but, the thing was, Vinnie owed me one. He owed me a big one. Vinnie and I had been fairly close buddies in high school. He'd been a year ahead of me, but we played on the same varsity basketball and baseball squads at Jackson Heights Senior, we'd been drinking pals, shot a lot of pool together, double-dated, shit like that. And I saved his ass one time. I really saved his butt from serious trouble one time, and he owed me. It was in the winter of senior year, February, 1953, on a Saturday night right after one of the home games. It was snowing like a bastard and we were on our way to the Astoria, a beer joint where we hung out a lot and played pool, up on Astoria Boulevard near Ninety-fourth Street. He was driving his father's car, and I remember the snow was so heavy you couldn't see for shit. We passed the Astoria, which was on the left, and Vinnie decided to hang a U-turn, since there was hardly any traffic. He was always hanging U-turns, as long as I'd known him, but he had good eyes and reflexes, he could handle anything on wheels, just like me. Anyway, this car came up behind us out of nowhere, speeding, tried to pass on our left just as Vinnie hooked into his turn. We almost missed him, he was going that fast. Vinnie's left front fender barely nicked the guy's right rear fender, but, going like he was, it spun him around at least twice, maybe three times, across the opposite lane, and he slammed into a parked bakery truck almost head-on. The man's name was Edward B. Hartman, and he lived on Lefferts Boulevard in South Ozone Park, Queens. He was fifty-seven years old. He died on the way to the hospital.

I testified that Vinnie had his directional signal turned on for a left turn off Astoria Boulevard into Ninety-fourth Street, which was about a hundred yards ahead. I was the only witness. Mr. Hartman's insurance company paid for the damage to Vinnie's father's car. It came to $129.12, mainly because the headlight was broken.

When I looked Vinnie up in the telephone book, I had to smile. After not seeing him for at least six years, probably closer to seven, the cheap son of a bitch still lived in the same old rent-controlled shithouse apartment on Sixty-ninth Street in Woodside, near the eastern end of New Calvary Cemetery. I remember you could see patches of that cemetery *and* patches of Lutheran Cemetery, to the south, from his living room windows. He must have lived there for a good fifteen years. Whenever I used to kid him about the view, he'd say I was dead right, but at least it was permanent. Something like that. He'd say, "You're dead right, Jackie-Boy, but at least the neighbors don't scream too much, huh?" The thing that used to break me up, he'd throw lines like that and always manage to keep his usual poker face and cold eyes. In basketball, whenever we were in a crisis situation, seconds left, time for maybe one play, his face would stay the same, expressionless, like he didn't have a nerve in his body. And it gave him the edge, more often than not. He was cold as ice. You could trust his judgment.

There was no answer the first four times I called, between about 8:30 and 9:15, but I finally got him at around 9:30. I found that my voice shook, I couldn't seem to control it. I didn't tell him anything except that I was in very serious trouble and needed to get out of the country immediately. He didn't ask a single question, just told me to give him an hour to make some calls, then call him back. When I rang him at 10:30, his line was busy. I got through about five minutes later, and he was very brief with me, saying he'd meet me right away. I gave him the address, Star Hotel, Northern Boulevard near 122nd Street. He said to be out front, packed, in half an hour.

I can remember standing in the dark, off to the side of the entrance, seeing my breath in the air, hearing the IRT trains roar past overhead. I'd put a bandage over the bridge of my nose, but it continued to throb like hell. Vinnie was about ten minutes late. Even at that time of night, jets kept taking off from LaGuardia, one around every forty-five seconds or so, passing to the north of

Shea Stadium, going almost directly over the hotel.

I was really glad to see Vinnie. As he paused in the dim light at the entrance, I could see he hadn't changed that much, except he'd grown a short mustache, and maybe added a few pounds. He wore a mackinaw, pulled open at the neck, showing a black knit tie. His eyes seemed as cold as ever, like brown glass.

I picked up my suitcase, walked toward him, managed a fast smile as we shook hands. We started walking through the alley.

"You've got a problem," he told me. "You're on the hit parade, kid."

I glanced at his eyes, didn't say anything.

"That priest got whacked was Carlo Ricci's brother. Forget the heat. Ricci went off his gourd. Got any money?"

"Couple thousand."

"What about a passport?"

"No."

"The two grand is your passport."

"Where am I going?"

"Get a train down to Baltimore. When you get there, go to Pier Forty-seven and ask at Customs for Nat Glick. Can you remember?"

"Yeah."

"Tell Nat you're a 'liberal-minded seaman.' And, Jackie, don't mention me, because right now I don't know you. I owed you a favor and this is it."

We had reached the other end of the alley, where Vinnie's car was parked. It was near one of the old-fashioned streetlights that you sometimes see in the older sections of Queens, and its dim glow made a yellow pattern on the top of the car. Vinnie gave me a quick slap on the arm to say good-by, walked around to the driver's side, opened the door.

"Where am I going?"

He paused, looked at me over the top of the car. His breath curled into the light, obscuring his eyes for just a moment. It happened again as he spoke. Softly: "I don't know that."

5

PORVENIR.

The Andes, that massive mountain system on the Pacific coast of South America, extend from Lake Maracaibo in northern Venezuela, all the way down through Colombia, Ecuador, Peru, Bolivia, Chile, and Argentina, a distance of some 4,500 miles, and the rugged peaks have an awesome quality even when you see them from the southernmost city in the world, Punta Arenas, Chile, approximately 4,100 miles below the equator, astride the Strait of Magellan, about equidistant from the Pacific and Atlantic. Porvenir doesn't qualify as a city, with only 2,127 inhabitants, but it's even further south, forty-five miles southeast across the Strait, on the Chilean side of an island named Tierra del Fuego (Land of Fire), a hellhole where the humidity is almost unbearable during the summer months, December through March. Yet, even in Porvenir, the Andes are rarely out of sight.

Although Chile's population of roughly 10 million includes 66 percent mestizo, 25 percent Spanish, and 5 percent Araucanian Indian, most residents of Porvenir are, strangely, of Yugoslavian descent, with a smattering of itinerant oil-field workers from other European countries, and a few from the United States. If you arrive by air from, say, Lima or La Paz, Rio or Buenos Aires, airport customs inspectors take a very close look at you, your passport, your visa, and your belongings, because Chile has been under the control of a military junta since 1973, supported by a wealthy elite with investments in commerce and industry, and the military live in constant fear of terrorist infiltration. But if you arrive aboard an oil tanker from Baltimore, with the unmistakable logo of COREPET (Compania de Recursos Petroleos), as Jackie Scanlon did, your visa and working papers are automatically in order.

Jackie Scanlon was never especially interested in American politics, much less those of another country, but even he was aware of the situation in Chile, because the American press did an overkill on the whole mess in the autumn of 1974. Although democratically elected Marxist President Salvador Allende was assassinated in the violent coup of September 11, 1973, it wasn't until a full year later that most of the world learned how heavily implicated the United States had been, through the CIA, which helped finance the growing military unrest with Allende. The U.S. was also involved with Chile's present economic crisis. Under the Allende government, inflation only went up 300 percent for the fiscal year ending in June, 1973; since the military took over, inflation was expected to reach 600 percent by the end of fiscal 1977. Worldwide criticism of the junta's continuing policies of imprisonment without trial, torture, and execution of former Allende supporters had become so vocal that the military actually—almost ludicrously—employed the U.S.-based J. Walter Thompson Company, largest independent advertising agency in the world, to counter the damaging publicity. JWT's image-building campaign lasted only one month; when several of the firm's overseas offices received threats of violence, the contract was cancelled.

Early Thursday morning, January 20, 1977, as Jackie slept in his tiny room at La Paloma Dulce, a workmen's hotel, top sheet clinging in the predawn heat, he experi-

enced the dream that had recurred periodically throughout his voyage on the oil
tanker, usually after his frequent bouts of
seasickness: What looked like a typical sixteenth-century Spanish galleon seemed to
have either run aground on fog-shrouded
rocks or was half-buried on the bottom of
the sea; he could never be certain. The
square-rigged sails on its three masts were
billowing in a raging storm or underwater
current, then started to rip apart, then shred,
the high bow and stern listing, straining. The
sound had changed from wind and water to
a distorted chorus of bell frogs combined
with the steady, unrelenting, mechanical
drone of unseen legions of insects.

What woke him was the scream of a pig
from the slaughterhouse down by the river.
Various animals were killed every morning
before dawn, before the real heat of the day
settled in, and the painful, hysterical cries
were impossible to shut out, and extremely
difficult to get used to. But you got used to
them. You had to. Pigs were always killed in
the little cement square outside the actual
slaughterhouse. The square was lighted by
wood fires in the corners, and filled with
farmers, kids, greedy dogs and cats. The
process was relatively simple. Each pig was
tied to a post, waiting its turn. When the

moment came, one man grabbed its hind legs and another man clubbed its head several times before introducing a long knife directly into the heart. Before it was removed, the knife was plunged a second time, and the man would quickly place his fingers into the wound to halt the flow of blood. After the stomach was opened, the two men would remove excess blood with cupped hands and pour it into cans. The remainder of the job was done primarily by kids. The skin was scrubbed with hot water before flaying, then the meat was taken out. For cows, the operation was performed inside the slaughterhouse.

Sitting up in bed, lighting his first cigarette, Jackie was relieved that the squealing had stopped. Again, he was aware of the continued, monotonous hum and buzz of insects, and the low, hoarse army of frogs. He threw off the damp sheet, went to the window, opened the louvered shutters; none of the hotel's windows had glass. The low buildings of the main street were in sharp silhouette against a gray sky. The air smelled of rain, as usual, but the pervading odor at that hour was rotting fruit. By midday, it would change to the heavy, penetrating, unmistakable smell of urine. Urine from dogs, cats, pigs, cows and mules, all together in the market; urine unable to sink into the always-muddy street, requiring many hours to evaporate in the constant humidity, despite the sun.

If you hung around Porvenir for only a week, the dominant impressions would not be those of poverty and filth and misery, which are always present, but those of paralyzing monotony and boredom. At 5:30 that morning, a little frog in the bathroom watched dully as Jackie pissed. Nobody was in the street yet, but in one of the bars, a nineteen-year-old whore named Serita was surrounded by three drunk men who punctuated their comments by caressing her body. She smoked, smiled, hummed the melody of the last record played on the jukebox two hours ago. She'd come out of her brothel the previous evening to freelance in the bars, and would return home in daylight with some food bought in the marketplace. She hoped to quit this town someday and work in one of the big brothels in Santiago.

At the same hour, the night watchman in the market square leaned his chair back against a store wall. In the pale yellow glow of his lantern, you could see that he wore a jockey cap, old coat, ragged pants, and you could hear the transistor radio in his lap, bringing early news and marimba music.

Down in the street, on long wooden planks over the mud, some goods left by sellers were dark bulks, looking like people sleeping. A dog sniffed the dark shapes suspiciously. A tripod of wooden poles, where sellers hung weights, now held broken dolls tied with wire.

Around 5:45, the first human shadow moved down the street: an old woman smoking her pipe and carrying a couple of saucepans. She unlocked the door of a small store, entered, quickly lighted a coal stove instead of switching on the lights, then began to boil something in one of the pans. You could see sparks of flame, and her shadow moved on the walls as she went to work. Far up the street, the silhouette of a small wagon moved slowly, pulled by a mule, driven by a man in a wide-brimmed hat. One of the wheels had a bad squeak. Three dogs walked behind. As the dark image squeaked closer to the market, you realized why the dogs were following. It was loaded down with the fresh carcasses of pigs. Behind the dogs, a tall man walked like a zombie, dragging the skin of a cow. When one of the dogs dropped back and grabbed the skin in its teeth, it stretched like rubber. Not far behind the tall man, a boy carried a cow's head to market; he held it on top of his head.

For the first few days, Jackie was tempted to think of all this as surrealistic, but the daily procession to market continued until dawn, and what had seemed haunting became commonplace, even monotonous, especially when the transistor radios started, one by one, building in numbers and volume, until it was no longer music but a caterwaul. Every kid in town had a transistor radio blaring, every housewife, every shopkeeper, every peddler, every whore. Surrealism? Even the little he knew about it seemed far too sophisticated for a shithole like this.

Before six o'clock, the headlights of three large trucks emerged from the road that led to the pumping station two miles away. Within minutes, scores of workers headed from their houses toward the main street, dressed in gray work clothes; a few wives carried cloth-wrapped bundles of food. Beyond the trucks, a soft orange glow was just beginning to define the massive peaks of the Andes to the east.

Jackie, dressed in work clothes, washed hurriedly near the shower area at the back of the hotel. In the hard light of the bare bulb over the mirror, his face seemed haggard, his eyes sunken, and he had a two-day growth of beard, because he hadn't allowed himself enough time to shave on Tuesday or Wednesday; he wouldn't have time today, either. The haircut he'd received from the so-called barber aboard the tanker was merely a short-back-and-sides job, altering his appearance for the worst, only starting to show signs of growing back. He didn't even attempt to comb it. As he passed the open window on the way back to his room, he glanced out automatically, as he'd done since Monday, to see if the strange old European man was there. He was, standing in the little backyard of his photographer's studio, smoking a cigarette that he held in that peculiar way, watching the glow above the mountains. His yard was clean and orderly, compared to the ones around it, and he wore a clean but threadbare undershirt, tucked into dark shorts that were too big around the waist. His white hair was trimmed almost neatly. The coconut palm tree he leaned against had a wide band of tin nailed around the middle of the trunk to prevent the rats from climbing up. Unaccountably, for the second straight morning, the man turned completely around and glanced up at Jackie, as if sensing his presence.

*   *   *

The long, flat clouds above the mountains had taken shades of red at 6:05, and swarms of flies buzzed around several chunks of meat that hung, dripping blood, in the outside kitchen just off the bar and dining area of El Corsario. Although euphemistically called a *taberna*, El Corsario was, in the grim reality of dawn, just a corrugated iron shack forming one side of a muddy courtyard, flanked on the other sides by three small "guesthouses," also constructed of corrugated iron, the zinc coating long since weathered, and all four structures were connected by long planks of heavy but rotting wood set in the black mud.

Victor Manzon, who occupied the guesthouse to the east of the courtyard, was shaving by the light of a small bulb hanging on a long wire above the mirror. Six days ago, when he moved in, the room was cluttered and rather dirty, but he'd managed to bring a small degree of order to it, and even some cleanliness. After shaving, brushing his teeth and combing his hair, he draped his towel over the foot of his bedstead, took his blue work shirt from the hook on the back wall near the window, put it on in front of the mirror. He'd lost weight over the past month, but in the right places, and his body looked harder than ever. He felt fit, which was essential, because he was doing the first manual labor he'd done since summer vacations from the Sorbonne, when he helped his father fish the Channel. He turned off the light, went out in the semidarkness, locked the door. He had only one valuable possession, hidden so well they'd have to tear the room apart, but the little lock on the door offered at least ostensible protection.

As he walked across the wooden planks, the mud of the courtyard reflected the first shafts of sunlight. He passed through the kitchen, smelled coffee brewing, then paused, as he had every morning that week, to look at the strange shrine outside the bedroom of Agrippa, the cook and waitress. On a wall facing east, under an overhanging section of corrugated roof, she'd hung a cemented collage of dozens of small animal skulls. It was a voodoo shrine that Carlos, the owner of the place, used as the butt of frequent jokes, but Victor admired it, especially in the unreal light of morning, when shadows changed its contours very subtly. Obviously, it had been created with infinite patience, and intuitive knowledge of design; an original piece of art in a village where any kind of art was in short supply.

Carlos was behind the bar, spraying insecticide. Known as Don Carlos to some of the locals, he was sixty-six, born and educated in Germany, but decades' of living in places like Porvenir had removed most of his Teutonic armor. He retained an accent, whether speaking Spanish or English, but that was it, with one notable exception. In the small of his back, tucked into his trousers and covered by sport shirts that always hung loosely, Carlos carried a prized possession, a very handsome, precision instrument: the classic Luger 9mm Standard Army, Model 1908, the automatic weapon officially adopted by the Ordnance Board for the German Army in World War II. It was manufactured by Deutsche Waffen-and-Munitionsfabriken, and intended for officers, after research questioned the necessity for the older safety grip on the regular Model '04-'06. It bore the year of manufacture (1943), stamped on the receiver directly ahead of the breechblock, together with the German government eagle, proof mark and serial number. None of these serial numbers ever ran very high; the official reason was that numbers would run so high it was more logical to start a new series every month. Therefore, a different letter of the alphabet was added to the end of the numbers every month. The last two numerals of Carlos's serial number were stamped on each individual part, and also stamped prominently on the outside of his weapon. Commercial model Lugers always had the outside numbers concealed for reasons of appearance.

"Good morning," Victor said in Spanish as he passed.

Carlos nodded. "Good morning, Herr Serrano."

Victor moved into the dining area, sat at his usual table, covered in oilcloth, set up with reasonably clean stainless-steel utensils, a paper napkin, coffee mug, small basket of bread, and a plate of butter. Flies swarmed around the butter. He shooed them away, broke off a piece of bread, buttered it, glanced at the pathetic, half-witted native boy who was sweeping the floor.

"Agrippa!" Carlos called toward the cook's room. "Bring some coffee for Herr Serrano."

Victor smiled when she finally came out and padded toward him, a dark-haired, dark-eyed Chilean in her middle forties, not especially attractive, but not homely, her figure difficult to determine in the usual loose dress, barefooted, walking in a way that just missed being graceful. They exchanged soft greetings as she poured the coffee from a battered enamel pot. She left the pot on the table, shooed the flies away from the butter, then smiled warmly and went back to the kitchen.

The half-witted boy finished his sweeping, picked up a can of fly spray, crossed to Victor's table, began spraying the butter.

"No," Victor told him. "Leave it, leave it."

Carlos turned, saw it, shouted at the boy.

The kid ducked his head automatically, as if to defend himself, crouched, walked away quickly.

Carlos leaned on the bar, regarded Victor with a helpless expression, tapped a finger to his temple.

"It doesn't matter," Victor said in German. "Are there any eggs today?"

Pleased, as usual, whenever Victor—or anybody—spoke his language, Carlos nodded and smiled. "Yes, Herr Serrano. Four-minute eggs?"

"Yes, please."

"Right away." He turned, started to relay the order in German, checked himself, smiling. "Agrippa, prepare two four-minute eggs."

* * *

At 6:30 that morning, when Kassem squinted at the sun, it seemed to undulate in sinuous, wavelike motions, an enormous red-orange sphere just clearing the jagged eastern peaks of the Andes. He was walking rapidly with nineteen other laborers, single-file along a path leading down to a series of catwalks over the swampy mud near the estuary. His cloth headband was already damp, his shirt and jeans were stiff with dried mud from the previous day's work, and the high rubber boots were at least a full size too big. He carried the same shovel that had made his hands almost numb for two days, digging trenches for the pipes that were being connected to the caisson, a structure consisting of an airtight chamber, open at the bottom, and containing air under sufficient pressure to exclude all water. It was the most backbreaking, tedious, boring labor he'd ever experienced, and he didn't know how much longer he could stand it. Most of the other men were used to it, mindless gorillas, accustomed to taking shouted orders and cheap crap from a foreman all day. Kassem had worked under foremen before, in construction labor during summer vacations, but this foreman, Zayas, was a real pig. Kassem had taken a silent, solemn oath that he'd either seriously injure or kill the son of a bitch, if he got half a chance. And, for the present, that thought, that possibility, kept him going.

Zayas, the stocky, fifty-four-year-old fore-man, born and raised in Porvenir, a third-generation Chilean of Yugoslavian descent, stood at the end of a dock that reached out over the muddy area where the men would be working. He watched as they fanned out, holding picks or shovels, trudged to the ends of the various catwalks, stepped off, sank into the thigh-deep black ooze, and slogged along toward the series of trenches that led to the caisson settings. He disliked Kassem for a number of reasons, primarily his superior attitude, so that morning he'd assigned him to work with a team that would have to hand-carry pipes through the trenches to the caisson. Digging was too easy for such an arrogant bastard. After a day of hauling pipe through the mud, he wouldn't feel so superior.

The team consisted of six men, one at either end of the long, heavy pipe, two on each side. They lifted the first section of pipe, began carrying it to the trench, as Zayas and his sub-foreman shouted orders. Kassem was on the right side, bent at the waist, both arms under the pipe, walking sideways through the deep mud, struggling with every step. About halfway to the caisson, he staggered to the side, throwing the other men slightly off balance. The pipe wavered back and forth, then fell heavily, splashing. All six men squirmed to regain their footing, and one of them was screaming, a young Araucanian Indian. As soon as he realized his leg was pinned under the pipe, he screamed louder, in short and long bursts, started clawing at the mud, and the others scrambled to their feet, grabbed for the pipe, tried desperately to lift it with mud-slick hands. Within seconds, they had it off him, and he was pushing himself back, crying with the pain. They could hear Zayas's whistle blowing.

"Leave him," the foreman ordered. "He's okay. Set the pipe. First set the pipe."

Kassem couldn't understand much Spanish, but he didn't have to. He followed the other men as they heaved the pipe to their shoulders this time, and moved ahead in the trench. Shaking with rage, he kept repeating a single phrase to himself, silently, in Arabic, mouthing it, spitting out the words, over and over, and it gave him the will to go on. When the pipe was finally set in the caisson, he looked back. Two laborers were lifting the Indian up on one of the catwalks, where a wheelbarrow was waiting. Zayas had been joined by two other men of the company's managerial group, *jefes*, but he was supervising, of course.

"Watch it, watch it, you idiots!" Zayas shouted to the laborers. "Can't you see this man is hurt?"

Kassem understood the tone, if not the words, and began repeating the Arabic phrase, silently, over and over, as he watched them place the Indian unceremoniously in the wheelbarrow. One of the laborers then pushed him slowly back over the catwalk toward a waiting pickup truck.

But when Kassem heard the plane in the distance, the first one he'd heard since he arrived, he stopped repeating the phrase and glanced up quickly, squinting. Several seconds later, when he caught sight of it, off to the south, flying relatively low, undoubtedly in an approach pattern for the airport, he tried to remember what that old heap had been called. He knew the classic, stubby lines of the fuselage, wings and tail, the two piston engines, the two front tires and one rear. What was it called? As it flew closer, losing altitude, its right side gleaming in the sun despite the mud-spattered, patched-up aluminum, he squinted har ̄ seeing the six square windows, remembering the dozens of photographs he'd seen in the Israeli newspapers and magazines, just last year, last June. Yes, yes, that was it. Last June, the highly-publicized fortieth anniversary of the legendary Douglas DC-3, the most famous piston-engined transport in aviation history. The inaugural flight had been in June, 1936, sixteen years before he was born.

Where was this old relic coming from? Who was it bringing to Porvenir? He knew COREPET was an American-owned multinational corporation, but details of its operations were extremely difficult to acquire. Fortunately, his foreign languages in school had been French and English, and, when he was in New York only two weeks ago, January 4-11, meeting with members of both Al Fatah and the PLO, who arranged his transportation, he'd heard and read the most sensational exposé on American-Chilean political relations to be uncovered since the coup of 1973. He'd read the article in the January 10 issue of *Newsweek,* titled "Man Without a Country," revealing the allegations of Edward Korry, former ambassador to Chile, and he'd seen Korry in a lengthy interview with Mike Wallace on the CBS-TV series "60 Minutes," Sunday, January 9.

Korry, ambassador to Chile from 1967 to 1971, planned to leave the United States permanently, to settle in France or Italy. Reason: in his judgment, Congress and the press had knowingly distorted the reasons for Salvador Allende's political downfall in 1973. While not questioning that Nixon plotted against Allende, through the CIA, Korry claimed that the Kennedy and Johnson Administrations, working with major

U.S. corporations, had actually set the precedent for serious U.S. interference in Chilean politics. Maintaining that Allende was corrupt, Korry went on to charge that Senator Frank Church's Senate Select Committee on Intelligence had engaged in a "flatly dishonest" cover-up of the facts, in an effort to preserve the reputations of Kennedy and Johnson, and protect the giant U.S. corporations involved. As a result of Korry's constant badgering of the Justice Department, a federal grand jury was now investigating sworn testimony about the Chilean situation made by officials of the CIA, and executives of at least one multinational corporation, for possible charges of perjury. Concerning his decision to leave the U.S. for good, Edward Korry said: "I love this country too much to live in it."

Kassem understood that sentiment, only too well. A man does what he has to do. If he goes along with the flood of political bullshit because he thinks he has too much to lose, he winds up losing the essence of the thing he loved. If he takes a stand against his own country, he may pay a very high price for that, too.

Squinting up at the old DC-3, wondering where it came from, and who might be on it, he recalled a line from Franz Kafka: "This village belongs to the Castle, and whoever lives here or passes the night here does so in a manner of speaking in the Castle itself. Nobody may do that without the Count's permission."

6

PRESIDENT IGNACIO LOPEZ GUITIERREZ didn't consider himself small at four feet seven inches, but other people did. Thus the physical abnormality had always been a serious psychological handicap. He understood the root cause of the problem. Normal people equated attractiveness with appearance only. Normal people accepted tangible reality. Normal people trusted the intuitive logic of sense perception. That's why normal people didn't understand power. From adolescence, he'd tended to overcompensate for his physical appearance by working much harder than others. At secondary school in Bonao, he'd finished third in a class of 154, and he'd majored in English at the University of Managua, before entering the army. Combining intelligence with discipline, obedience, and monomaniacal attention to detail, he'd been promoted to the rank of major at age twenty-four, lieutenant colonel at twenty-nine, brigadier general at thirty-three, and full general at forty-one. With the financial assistance of major U.S. multinational corporations, and strategic advice of the CIA, Guitierrez orchestrated the military unrest that eventually led to the assassination of Juan Ramón in the coup of September, 1973. He appointed himself president the same month, at the age of forty-seven.

Who ruled his country? In theory, it was a republic with a 1964 constitution providing for a president and bicameral legislature to be elected every four years. In fact, since independence in 1841, the country had an uninterrupted history of dictators, coups, countercoups, assassinations, and military rulers. Who really ruled? Both historically and through its present investment interests, the U.S. played a dominant role. Oshawa Copper, a Canadian-based, U.S.-operated mining concern, had opened a $150 million mining-refining complex; Texas-Western had extensive interests in sugar and tourism; COREPET had built a $30 million oil refinery. In the past two years, Guitierrez had established five "free zones" where U.S. firms could operate free of taxes for up to twenty-five years, while they exploited the cheap labor and the absence of unions.

Guitierrez understood the causal relationships of power much better than most military men. The basics remained the same; Power was achieved by force or force-potential; dissent was checked by imprisonment, torture, execution, and the constant threat of same; control was maintained by a careful duality of paternal concern and enforcement. Trust was accomplished by far more subtle means, persuasive behavior that Guitierrez was still studying. It required communication of an extremely sophisticated nature.

One of his teachers was COREPET; specifically, John Webber, senior vice-president of the Latin American Division, whose textbook, *A Psychology of Corporate Communication,* was considered the definitive work in its field, required reading at many U.S. business schools, and whose many gifts over the past three years had included a Hughes YOH-6A helicopter with an Allison T-63-A-5 engine, a Xerox 9200 Duplicating System, an IMSAI desk computer, a Lear jet, a Jaguar XJ12C, and a bulletproof eight-passenger Cadillac limousine. But the gift that had continued to hold Guitierrez's attention on a day-to-day basis was one of the simplest: a COREPET teletype machine. Every COREPET office, worldwide, had at least one teletype machine (the major offices had one for every middle- and top-management executive), and every workday a series of complicated messages would be sent from the corporate headquarters in Baltimore. All communications were in English. All important orders and instructions to the Latin American Division were sent by Webber. After three years of study, Guitierrez had advanced to the stage of understanding the price-cost probabilities of transactions and investments in COREPET's vast multinational dominion of petro-dollars, and he was presently trying to unravel its statistical decision theories, linear programming charts, and minimax solutions. The element that intrigued him most about the messages from Webber was the complex subliminal psychology at work. Guitierrez was well aware that the common denominator of all humanity was insecurity; it was an axiom of critical importance in his rise to power. Fear was among the most primitive emotions known to man. Illogical. Irrational. Incomprehensible. If you were interested in a common vulnerability to assuage, what could be better?

On Thursday morning, January 20, Guitierrez entered his lavishly appointed office in the Presidential Palace to find the first message of the day clicking softly across the paper behind the glass window of the gray teletype machine by his desk. The only symbol identifying the machine was a small metal plate on the front with the COREPET logo, the condor.

HQ 1-20 0835
CORLETTE CHIEF OPER POZA RICA
SUBVERSION AND TERRORISM BY EXTREMISTS ACTING IN CONTEMPT OF THE GOVERNMENT REQUIRES THAT WE IMPOSE MAXIMUM SECURITY MEASURES. EFFECTIVE IMMEDIATELY CMA IN COOPERATION WITH CIVIL AND MILITARY AUTHORITIES CMA INCREASE SECURITY PATROL TO 12 REPEAT 12. BUDGET ALLOCATED. CONFIRM SOONEST.
—WEBBER

* * *

Victor saw the DC-3 make its final approach over the huge crude-oil storage tanks of the refinery. Sweating, he stood by the side of a mud-caked solvent truck and helped a man named Marquez unreel a heavy hose, pulling and straining, while the other ten men in the group lugged the hose and high-pressure nozzle toward one of the storage tanks. Marquez glanced at the plane, too, eyes narrowed in the shade of his hardhat. A fair-haired, fair-skinned, muscular man of fifty-seven, he looked even more German than his old friend Carlos, despite the thin beard that appeared white in the sun, and his accent was certainly more pronounced. But he spoke Spanish fluently, as well as French.

Jackie Scanlon and Spider Nicholson watched the DC-3 from another angle, sitting on the front fenders of their truck at the airport, ready to pick up equipment for the refinery and a new generator that was arriving. Spider was an ex-longshoreman from Boston who'd crippled a Teamster official in 1973, and he'd been with COREPET two years. They were parked next to the squat, dilapidated structure that served as the airport terminal. Two of its walls were reinforced by strips of aluminum fuselage, and the hand-painted wooden sign on the roof held peeling capital letters. AEROPUERTO PORVENIR. Since the arrival of any plane was something of a curiosity (an average of one flight a week), a crowd of ten adults and sixteen children had gathered near the fence. Two *agentes de policía* in worn khaki uniforms were already seated at a card table on the wooden walkway leading to the shack, and two black men stood behind them, both wearing black hats, blood-red neckties against black shirts, black trousers and shoes, traditional dress of the *tonton macoute*, practitioners of *obeah*. An ancient bus was parked behind the shack, next to two flatbed trucks, a *policía* car, and the only cab in town, a mud-spattered 1963 Chevrolet with the word TAXI badly hand-painted on the driver's door, where the COREPET logo had been painted over.

Seeing the DC-3 roar in slowly to land on the single, narrow, muddy strip of runway, with kids yelling, Jackie felt the same emotion he'd been experiencing since he heard about the flight: a nagging, sickening, almost paranoid fear of arriving strangers. The plane needed the full length of the runway to stop. It turned and taxied back toward the shack, nose held high, propellers flashing in the sun, passing a little cinderblock hangar enclosed by a cyclone fence with the COREPET logo. Even from a hundred yards away, Jackie could see how battered the plane really was, patched and dented, discolored, a relic from a different age.

Nobody guided it in to park, of course, and there weren't even any wheel blocks. Its little rear tire just turned it toward the shack, then turned it again, passenger door facing the crowd; the pilot revved the engines loudly before shutting them off, and the propellers were still spinning as two teenage boys rolled out the five-step ramp. Spider drove toward the rail, made a U-turn along the fuselage, then backed up slowly to the cargo door at the side. When he stopped, Jackie got out, guided him back the last few feet, then watched the passenger door through the wooden slats of the truck bed. Nine men and one woman disembarked, all poorly dressed, carrying rope-tied baggage and cardboard boxes. After a few minutes, when no one else appeared, Jackie placed one foot on the rear tire, grabbed the lowest slat, and was about to pull himself up. He froze in that position.

The man's shoes were white, clean, expensive-looking, and the cuffed trousers of his white silk suit held a sharp, almost perfect crease. As he walked down the steps, Jackie co⸱ .d see his suit coat, spotless, virtually un-wrinkled, natural shoulders, medium-wide lapels, buttoned, meticulously tailored, obviously custom-made, revealing the narrow waistline. His dark-blue shirt was open at the neck, and he wore very dark sunglasses under a black, narrow-brimmed hat. His mustache was gray in contrast to his pure-white hair, and the rawboned face had a pale copper complexion, the kind that so often signaled a failing liver. He held a small leather valise, and walked to the side of the ramp, glancing around casually, giving the distinct impression that he was merely in transit. When he looked at the back of the truck, his dark glasses made it difficult to tell if he actually saw Jackie between the wooden slats, but his head paused momentarily before turning to watch the pilot come down the ramp. He nodded to the pilot, placed a fist to his mouth as he coughed softly. For several minutes, he stood almost motionless, observing the crowd, the *policía* checking passports at the card table, the cars and trucks parked near the fence. In his profession, he was known only as "Nilo." No one who had been associated with him for the past twenty-two years ever knew if that was his first ɑr last name.

Jackie climbed up on the truck quickly, went into the cargo section, helped Spider shove the crate with the generat⁀ to the door. As soon as they maneuvered it to the edge, Spider squeezed past it, jumped down to operate the hydraulic lift. Alone in the plane for a minute, Jackie took a good look at the passenger section.

Spider's voice startled him. "Forget it. If you stop eating, a year's pay might get you a seat to the next rathole."

Jackie grabbed the sides of the crate, helped wrestle it out on the lift. When it was in place, he rode the lift down, glanced at the man in the white suit, who had moved close to the line of people in front of the card table.

The police were very methodical. The older one examined every page of every passport, read every stamp, studied every visa. The younger one, who didn't look much older than some of the teenagers standing around, opened every piece of luggage, every box, took every single item out. Every jar, tube or bottle that looked like it might contain medicine was handed to the two black men with the red neckties, who examined each with utmost curiosity. A uniformed but unshaven employee of the airline stood nearby, holding a handful of ragged cards marked with bold letters: TRÁNSITO.

Nilo smoked a cigarette, observed for a while longer. In all the years he'd been traveling, he'd never witnessed such a slow, plodding, inexperienced inspection. He took a final drag on the cigarette, dropped it, stepped on it. Stifling a cough, he walked over to the unshaven airline employee.

"I'm in transit," he told the man.

"*Que?*"

"*Tránsito.*" He pointed to himself. "I'm going to Managua."

"*Ah, Managua, si.*" The man handed him a card.

As Nilo passed the card table, the older

officer held up his hand, looked him up and down.

"*Tránsito*," Nilo said, showed him the card. "Can I get something to drink?"

The *oficial* frowned, moved his hand to shoo several flies.

Nilo held up an imaginary glass, made a drinking motion.

"*Pasaporte?*" The man picked up a fly-swatter, stared at a fly that had just alighted on the table.

"In the plane. With my baggage."

The *oficial* shrugged, kept his eyes on the fly. He raised the swatter, aimed carefully, slammed it dead.

"I'm very thirsty." Nilo reached into his trouser pocket, slid a fifty-peso note behind the transit card, turned it so only the *oficial* could see it."

"*Pase.*" The man tapped the fly from the swatter, scraped the bill toward him.

Nilo walked casually to the window on the east side of the shack where soft drinks were sold, paused, then continued around the building to the muddy 1963 Chevrolet with the word TAXI hand-painted on the door. He tossed his small valise in back, got in, closed the door quietly, told the driver to take him into town. As the taxi pulled away, he sat back calmly, removed the transit card from his inside coat pocket, tore it into extremely small pieces.

*　*　*

HQ 1-20 0955
LARTIGUE MAN DIR PORVENIR
PREVIOUSLY ANNOUNCED FUEL
SHORTAGE EASTERN TWO-
THIRDS U.S. NOW CRITICAL.
EMERGENCY REQUIRES NEW
DEADLINE 2-28 REPEAT 2-28 RE
YOUR 160 THOUSAND BARRELS.

EFFECTIVE IMMEDIATELY CMA
MANAGEMENT/SPECIALIST EM-
PLOYEES ELIGIBLE ADMINISTRA-
TIVE OVERTIME CMA PER
COREPET REG. 532-3. DOUBLE-
TIME RATE AUTHORIZED ALL
HOURS WORKED WEEKENDS. DE-
TAILS SHOULD BE PERSONALLY
EXPLAINED TO ALL EMPLOYEES
AFFECTED CMA URGENCY
STRESSED. —WEBBER

7

IN THE LATE AFTERNOON, summer rain drummed metallically on the corrugated roof of El Corsario's *taberna*, mercifully drowning out the incessant merengue music on the radio, and, from the shadowed bar, Nilo watched the heavy drops bounce and spray in the muddy courtyard. He took a long swallow of Scotch, clinked the ice, watched the liquid swirl; then a luxurious drag on the cigarette and a slow exhale toward the ceiling, eyes narrowing as smoke curled into the shafts of light. From the moment he'd walked in, about an hour before, his face had struck a quick, vague spark somewhere back in Carlos's mind. It was a face you couldn't easily forget, the kind of face Marquez might call *ungewöhnlich*, weather-beaten and with deep lines from nostrils to chin, eyes sunken, lids half-drawn, mustache almost concealing the wrinkled upper lip, tilted hat now revealing a bald pate. He was extremely soft-spoken, calm, polite, apparently a very private man, not inclined to exchange small talk. Where had he seen that face before? Carlos's mind continued to grope for a few minutes, names and places and years spinning. But the face drew a blank.

When Nilo finished the drink, Carlos led him through the kitchen; he'd asked to see one of the guest rooms. As they passed Agrippa's room, Nilo paused, attracted by the shrine. Rain poured off the overhang of the roof, catching the light at an angle that partially obscured the animal skulls. Nilo studied them, massaged the bridge of his nose. Agrippa was just around the corner, loading wood into the small stove. The retarded native boy sat in the corner near a pile of rubbish, slowly plucking the feathers from a decapitated chicken.

As they entered the courtyard, Nilo's suit seemed almost incandescent against the soft rain and black mud. He followed Carlos along the wooden plank leading to the shack at the south side of the yard.

"I have three rooms, but one is taken." Carlos indicated the lights in Victor's window. The door was slightly ajar, throwing a very thin yellow ribbon across the slick mud.

Victor sat on the edge of the bed, tired and depressed, staring vacantly at the bare floor. Hearing Carlos, he stood up slowly, walked to the door, squinted out. His shadow was long and narrow, bending through the puddles. Nilo observed it.

Carlos reached the room on the south side, stood under the little roof, turned the doorknob both ways. It was locked. He cursed softly, then called across the courtyard in Spanish: "Agrippa, bring me the key."

Nilo waited with him under the roof, looked around casually, unperturbed at the filth of the place. He coughed, put a fist to his mouth, coughed again, noted that Victor's figure was still in the doorway, motionless. He listened to the rain, watched it spray sideways in the breeze.

Agrippa had to go to her room for the key. Instead of walking on the planks, she slopped barefoot through the mud. She smiled at Nilo as she approached, rain glistening on her face, handed Carlos the key.

He unlocked the door, swung it open, turned on the lights, motioned for Nilo to enter.

Nilo didn't go in. "I'll take it."

"For how long?"

He glanced around the courtyard, seeing Victor's shadow, and paused, listening to the rain. "Let's say a week."

❋ ❋ ❋

Before twilight, the rain had moved on, helped by a brisk southeast wind from the sea. Slender, graceful clouds in the west were streaked red above the dark mountains, and the color was reflected in the river, brightened to vermilion for a brief time, then faded to soft shades of orange with the oncoming dusk. Large puddles in the main street mirrored the same colors, like smoked glass, and a procession of dark figures moved across them, slowly, returning from the marketplace as inexorably as they had arrived, people, cows, mules, goats, pigs, each at the same plodding pace, an occasional cart or truck overtaking them, splashing softly. Transistor radios were still playing merengue, but not quite as loudly then, as if by tradition, until nightfall. The rain and wind had long since changed the familiar midday smell of urine back to rotting fruit, and, in the narrow alleys of the slums near the river, the odor of cooking fish was already penetrating.

Victor became aware of that smell gradually as he followed his little "guide," a boy of about twelve, from El Corsario through a series of alleys and into a part of town where, in the dusk, oil lamps began glowing in the windows of the shacks. His degree of poverty didn't give him acceptance here; many of the people he passed looked at him in an unfriendly way. He was obviously a foreigner, an *extranjero*, and, in some vague way, responsible for part of the misery. Men were returning from work, a few on mules; other men passed in small groups on their way to the bars. A small man with eyeglasses struggled along, completely bent over, carrying two large sacks on his back. Dogs and pigs wandered in the narrow lanes between the shacks. Up one of the lanes, Victor saw a woman with a candle opening the door of an outhouse.

The boy walked a few steps ahead of Victor, puffing one of the cigarettes he'd been given as payment, obviously pleased with his assignment. As they approached the main street, they passed a man on homemade crutches, dragging a huge elephantiasis-ridden leg. The boy went to the entrance of the photographer's shack, one door in from the main street, next to the three-story La Paloma Dulce workmen's hotel. He knocked hard, waited, looking at his cigarette. A sullen-looking woman appeared at the door. After a brief exchange of fast, incomprehensible Spanish, the boy motioned for Victor to wait over at the side.

La Palma Dulce was one of the few structures in the area that had electric lights. Its rear windows threw angular patterns across the lane and Victor could see the drooping leaves of the coconut palm tree in the photographer's little backyard, and a glint of something metal on its trunk. A shadow moved on the back porch of the hotel; a man sat there, smoking, looking down at him. Victor could only see one side of his face, but he recognized him instantly as one of the American workers who hung around the bar of El Corsario.

He held the man's gaze for a few seconds, then heard the voices of two men at the photographer's front door, turned, and went back. The two men were leaving, and the boy smiled and waved him inside. A dog growled as he entered.

The small front room was relatively dark, illuminated by a single oil lamp, but he could see a man seated on a bed against the side wall. The boy indicated a chair just inside the door. Victor sat down, squinting, and the boy sat between the men, hushed the dog that was still snarling. As Victor's eyes adjusted, the man leaned forward on the bed, closer to the lamp, revealing neatly trimmed white hair, deep-set eyes, and a rather gaunt face with severe lines accentuated by the shadows.

"Comprende inglés?" Victor asked softly.

"Yes. I speak some." His accent was difficult to determine, sounded central European.

The boy lit his second cigarette from the first one.

"You want to travel away?" the man asked.

"Yes."

"I can fix for you . . . *a la capital.*"

Victor lit a cigarette, inhaled deeply. "I want to go out of this country."

The man raised his eyebrows, changed his tone of voice to one of surprise. "Out from this country? *Difícil.* Very difficult."

"Impossible?"

"No . . . *es posible.*" He groped for a word. "*Costoso. Comprende?* Cost much."

"*Comprendo.*"

In the pause, they avoided each other's eyes, heard the sound of distant merengue music. Victor saw the dog under one of the chairs.

The boy took a drag on his cigarette, watched the old man's face, enjoying the whole thing. "*Tiene un reloj de oro puro.*"

"*Déjame verlo,*" the man told him. "*Traémelo.*"

Turning to Victor, the boy tapped his wrist. "*El reloj.*"

Victor nodded, hesitated, then pulled up his sleeve and removed the gold Lucien Piccard. The boy stood up, kept the cigarette in his mouth as he handed it to the old man.

The merengue music became progressively louder as someone walked past the door with a transistor radio, then gradually softened. The old man held the watch to the lamplight as he examined it slowly, with a practiced eye, front and back. He strapped it on his wrist, admired it, then spoke to the boy in a fast Spanish vernacular that Victor couldn't follow. The kid answered even faster, smiling.

Finally, the man glanced at Victor. "I can fix it for you to go out from the country." He tapped the face of the watch. "This *reloj*, plus one thousand pesos."

Victor took a deep breath, shook his head slowly. "I have only the watch."

The old man shrugged.

＊　＊　＊

At 7:20 that night, the smoke-filled *taberna* of El Corsario was jammed with workmen who had only a limited time to get drunk on the beer and cheap rum, and were swilling it, voices raised to a pitch that nearly obliterated the merengue blast from the jukebox. Sitting at the end of the bar, Jackie seemed oblivious to the noise, cutting a very tough piece of meat, shoveling it into his mouth, washing it down with beer, rereading sections of his torn, yellowing, December 13, 1976, issue of the *New York Daily News*. Carlos glanced at Jackie's food and beer, added up the bill, counted to himself in German.

"Four pesos, twenty centavos," he announced loudly.

Chewing, smiling, Jackie pulled out a five peso note, handed it to him. "Give me another beer. I'm celebrating."

Carlos scribbled *pagado* on the bill. "What occasion?"

"The end of my dry season."

As Carlos went for the new bottle, Jackie leaned against the bar, stared up at the old-fashioned Coca-Cola poster on the wall. It was from the 1940s, and he remembered seeing identical ones as a kid: the typical blonde, shapely, all-American girl in a swimsuit, lying on the beach, smiling with perfect white teeth, reaching for an ice-cold, sweating bottle of Coke.

Victor came in, sat at the end of the bar to Jackie's left.

Carlos returned with the beer, nodded to him. "And Herr Serrano, what would you like?"

"Ein whiskey."

Crossing to the cupboard behind the bar, Carlos removed a half-full quart of Johnnie Walker Red Label. He smiled at the sight of it, came back with an expression of obvious pride, showing the label.

Victor pursed his lips. "I haven't seen that down here before."

"Private stock." He pointed to the lower

left portion of the label that read *86.8 Proof*. "Very rare." After inspecting a glass to be sure it was clean, he poured carefully.

"Put it on *my* account," Jackie told him.

Victor turned, hesitated, then nodded. Jackie gave a nod in return, mopped up his gravy with a piece of bread, went back to reading his newspaper.

"You're in the workers' hotel?" Victor asked.

"I like the view."

"Yes, I thought about it myself. Twenty centavos a day, isn't it?" He tried the Scotch.

Jackie stuck the bread in his mouth, licked his fingers, nodded. He chewed quickly, took a drink of beer. "I understand you used to be in banking."

"Oh?"

"That's the rumor."

"I had no idea I was the subject of rumors."

"Carlos used to be an ex-*Reichsmarschall*. Right, Carlos?"

Carlos gave him a cold glance.

Victor took another drink. "What's your profession, Mr.—?"

"Dominguez," Jackie said, smiling.

"—Dominguez?"

"Ice hockey."

Victor inclined his head to the side,

glanced at his drink, clinked the ice, then took a long swallow, finishing it.

"Carlos, bring Mr. Serrano another whiskey."

"Let me get this," Victor said.

"No, tonight I'm a sport," Jackie mopped up the last of his gravy. "Read about this place in a travel brochure?"

"I heard it had a healthy climate."

"And it wasn't what you expected."

"It was *exactly* what I expected."

Carlos poured the Scotch carefully, left the bottle near Victor, walked to the opposite end of the bar to join his friend Marquez, who was talking with Kassem.

Victor downed the Scotch in three swallows, poured himself another, decided to drink it in one go, then sat back smiling, savoring the long, deep burn.

"I think he figured you'd sip that," Jackie said. His attention was drawn to two police *oficials* coming in the door. They were better dressed than the ones at the airport, wore clean khaki uniforms and brown trooper-style hats with wide brims. Their gunbelts supported well-polished holsters with flaps, and the wraparound cartridge loops held copper-jacketed .45-caliber slugs. They walked slowly down the bar, where they were greeted coolly by Carlos. After asking a few brief questions, they both turned, looked directly at Jackie, walked slowly toward him.

The heavier one, Captain Montalvo, wore steel-rimmed glasses, spoke quietly. "Juan Dominguez?"

Jackie concentrated on pouring his beer, didn't answer.

"*Oiga!*" Lieutenant Gaitán demanded. "*Le estamos hablando.*" He was loud, stocky, with a thick mustache.

Jackie put his beer down, looked at him. "*No comprendo.*"

Around the bar, conversation softened quickly, then stopped. Chairs and stools scraped as men maneuvered for a better view, or left. Merengue music continued monotonously from the jukebox. Carlos hurried down the bar, removed the bottle of Johnnie Walker.

Victor stood up, started to leave.

"*Quédate!*" Lieutenant Gaitán told him. He inclined his head toward Jackie. "*Es amigo tuyo?*"

Victor glanced at Jackie. "No." He turned, walked away.

Captain Montalvo spoke English, treated Jackie with an air of condescension. "You don't understand? Let's see your identity card."

Jackie frowned. "*Como?*"

He tapped Jackie's shirt pocket. "The

identity card that you keep here." He took the card out, read it. Behind the steel-rimmed glasses, his brown eyes seemed permanently sad. They remained so even when he smiled, cleared his throat, and read the card aloud, for the benefit of everyone in the bar. "Let's see, 'Juan Dominguez. Born: November twenty-five, nineteen thirty-nine, in Las Columnas.' That is *you*?" He studied Jackie's face. "You don't *look* like you were born in Las Columnas."

Jackie played it straight. *"Porque no?"*

"Because you don't even speak Spanish. And because you're a filthy . . . gringo . . . *asshole!"*

Lieutenant Gaitán shook his head. *"Es un asunto serio."*

"This is forged," Montalvo said. "It's a violation of the immigration laws." He snapped his holster open, stepped back, hands ready at his sides.

Gaitán barked ritualistic orders at Jackie in Spanish. It was the full search-and-arrest number, learned from American police training films, played to the accompaniment of brassy jukebox merengue. Jackie responded wearily, stood, braced his hands against the edge of the bar, spread his legs. Gaitán did a snappy but cautious frisk, then grabbed his shoulders, pushed him to the door.

As he was shoved across the veranda toward the *policía* car, Jackie's eyes were involuntarily drawn to the luminescence of the white silk suit worn by the man who was leaning against the corrugated wall, smoking calmly in the dark.

Ten minutes later, two black men stood by the dimly lighted entrance of the *estación de policía*, wearing the uniform of the *tonton macoute*. They exchanged familiar nods with Montalvo and Gaitán as Jackie was escorted inside. A third *oficial* followed them along a damp corridor flanked by twelve filthy, iron-barred detention cells. They were all occupied, three to a cell, and all the men were naked.

When they reached the small, cluttered office, Montalvo hung his hat carefully on a rack, opened an old-fashioned refrigerator that had circular coils on top, removed a bottle of Coca-Cola. Jackie was positioned under the glare of a hanging bulb in the center of the room, as Gaitán stood behind him, reached into his pockets, emptied the contents on a desk. The only money he found was a single bill and some change.

He turned Jackie around. "*Más? No tienes más?*"

Montalvo sat on the edge of the desk, took out his .45 automatic, used the hammer as a bottle opener. "You have more?"

Jackie shrugged, "That's it."

Gaitán handed the money to Montalvo, smiled. *"Que cabron ese . . . no tiene plata."*

Montalvo laughed softly, sipped the Coke. "Okay, next time, you pay—" he held up three fingers, then one. "Earn three, we take one." He put the money in his pocket. *"Comprendo?"*

"Comprendo."

He motioned with the bottle. "Okay. *Fuera.*"

Jackie gathered up his belongings. "I need my card."

"Qué?" Gaitán asked. *"Fuera!"*

"I can't work without my card. *Mi tarjeta.*"

"A la tarjeta, sí." Gaitán took the card from Montalvo, made a digging motion with it before handing it to Jackie. *"Para trabajar. Y para ganar."* He laughed loudly, rubbed his fingers together.

Jackie put the card in his shirt pocket, walked to the door.

Captain Montalvo smiled, imitated Jackie's accent. *"Adiós, Señor Dominguez."*

124

8

THE COREPET TELETYPE MACHINE in Charles Corlette's office started clicking at 7:18 a.m., Friday, January 21, but no one was there to read it. As chief of operations at Mariette 1, the new COREPET oil field in Poza Rica, 218 miles northwest of Porvenir, Corlette was entitled to the machine by reason of his management grade, but it looked as out of place in the stark, cluttered, dirty corrugated structure as the electric typewriter on a stand near his desk, a typewriter he'd never used once since he was transferred from the field in Trinidad four years ago. Outside, the noise of generators, drills, cranes and trucks had already reached the level that necessitated shouting for the most simple communication, and Corlette was out there in the thick of it, yelling. That's the way he communicated with his eighty-three men. Things like teletype machines and typewriters were for men like his boss, Georges Lartigue, managing director back at the refinery in Porvenir, whose calm, soft-spoken, business-school approach to the corporate political intrigues of CORE-PET placed him worlds apart—fortunately—from crude jungle clearings like Poza Rica, where the real action took place. Mariette 1 was for strong, direct, hardhat bosses, and young workers who knew how to take orders. Here, you started work at 7:00 sharp, broke for lunch at exactly noon, quit at 4:30, lined up for chow in the commissary at 5:30, played a few simple games, got drunk, and hit the sack in the barracks early—because you were physically beat.

At 7:18, as the teletype clicked away, teams of men and equipment moved over the plank road, still under construction, that would interconnect the five wells. A group of riggers was replacing the casing on one well, working in a kind of rhythmic ballet as the huge crane lifted lengths of pipe high into the derrick, then placed them into a spinning bit to be driven into the ground. Another group was swarming over a large tree they'd just felled at the edge of the jungle, hacking off branches with machetes, moving in with chain saws. A total of twelve armed guards kept watch atop four twenty-foot towers on all sides of the field.

Corlette, a tall, heavyset, fifty-two-year-old American with a slight beer belly, was walking toward one of the diesel trucks, discussing a set of plans with Mort Cooper, his American foreman, whose hair was prematurely white, and whose accent was decidedly deep south.

"What about yield?" Corlette yelled over the noise.

"I think it should produce twice as much as this last one that we just come out of."

"When can you get this one pinched off?"

"Just as soon as we perforate—"

The base of the new well exploded with the force of a full case of nitroglycerin, blew men and debris in all directions; instantly, the ground shook as a geyser of flaming oil shot up through the derrick. Before it billowed into a red mushroom, ground vibrations detonated single cases of nitro planted in locations within a radius of 300 feet; seven explosions occurred in a chain-reaction. Men outside the critical radius were shouting and running wildly. Others, like Corlette and Cooper, crouched in stunned disbelief, watched the new derrick collapse into the roaring funnel. Corlette saw two young workers down on the plank road near the blaze; one was screaming and trying to drag himself out, the other was on fire, rolling over and over, hysterical with the pain. Corlette and Cooper ran toward them, but the heat was too intense. They stopped, retreated, looked back. The man on fire had stopped rolling. The other man's clothes had ignited and he was running blindly toward the geyser. Men were screaming and crying. The area was littered with dead, burned and injured.

During the next half hour, Corlette's experience in similar fires turned utter chaos into a semblance of organization. He sent all twelve guards out to search the area; assigned teams to spray foam with high-pressure hoses from four sides of the fire, to prevent ignition of the capped wells; supervised the loading of two trucks to transport the six dead and thirteen seriously burned men to Porvenir; called Lartigue, asked for a chartered plane to get the burned men from Porvenir to Bonao, and suggested that the Bonao General Hospital be alerted to prepare its emergency facilities for burn victims.

At 8:05, just before the trucks left for Porvenir, six of the guards returned. They had found the remains of a guerrilla camp less than a mile away, brought back part of a detonator with the wire still attached, plus two large cans covered in oilpaper with Chinese writing. Corlette placed Cooper in charge of emergency treatment for the twenty-two workers with superficial burns and minor injuries, assigned three guards to each truck, then got in his Jeep and preceded the trucks into Porvenir. Despite the poor road, which he'd driven hundreds of times, he averaged forty-five miles per hour, and made it to the refinery before one o'clock.

* * *

The teletype machine occupied a conspicuous position next to Georges Lartigue's teakwood desk, and his office was relatively large, adequately furnished with the status symbols of a COREPET managing director —dictaphone, refrigerator, bar, couch, coffee table—but the décor was nondescript, unimaginative to the point of drabness. His faded blue walls held no paintings or prints, just a few photographs in black wooden frames, including a formal portrait of President Guitierrez, next to three equally cold black-and-white public relations shots of COREPET's president, executive vice-president, and senior vice-president of the Latin American Division; no photographs of the board of directors had ever been released, and the chairman's actual identity was unknown.

Although Lartigue was American, his fluency in French and Spanish had resulted in lengthy field assignments in Martinique,

Guadeloupe, Puerto Rico and Santiago, investing his English with permanent overtones of the other two languages. Bald, thin, he wore rimless glasses, and his spotless white sport shirt accentuated a deep bronze tan, making him look a bit younger than his sixty-one years.

Corlette's face seemed sunburned as he came in and slammed a large paper bag on the desk. He removed the section of detonator with the wire attached, then the two cans with the Chinese writing.

Lartigue picked up the detonator, examined it carefully. "Very professional."

"Well, get it to the *capital* and maybe we'll get some *results!*"

Lartigue walked to the bar, spoke quietly as he poured two glasses of Scotch. "The government's been told it's an accident."

"*What?*"

"Charles, in this country, terrorists who blow up American oil wells are heroes."

"We're paying that government to give us *protection!*"

Lartigue handed him a glass. "El Presidente cannot risk his liberal image by sending his troops to chase patriots."

"Christ."

After crossing to his desk and sitting, Lartigue picked up a yellow paper. "This is a Telex from home, in response to my report.

The first part just concerns 'regret loss of life,' et cetera, et cetera, 'injuries,' and so on. And, apparently, we have no insurance position because of the sabotage thing. Anyway, this is the part that concerns you: 'Limitations on production in recent months due to acts of terrorism and political uncertainties *emphasize* attention immediate supply obligations with minimum concern R and D.'"

Corlette went to the window, leaned against the wall that held a neat row of clipboards with schedules. "What the hell is R and D?"

"Research and development. 'Please advise course of action soonest.'"

In the pause, Corlette sipped his drink. "Is that it?"

"Yes."

Corlette took a deep breath, sighed. "What're the immediate supply obligations?"

"One tanker of one hundred and sixty thousand barrels by the end of next month. We *need* that well to fill it."

"They'll have to delay it."

As Lartigue leaned back, his chair scraped against the section of wall that had a deep horizontal scar from thousands of similar leanings. "They can't. The charter is running. If we have to take a loss that big, we might as well shut down now and save expenses."

* * *

At 1:35 that afternoon, when the two truckloads of dead and burned workers arrived in Porvenir, over three hundred people were waiting in the square. Transistor radios had various news broadcasts on, producing a strange pattern of sound. As the trucks came closer, coated with dust, splashing mud, three armed guards standing behind each cab, the crowd moved toward them slowly, then faster as the momentum took hold, people pushing, shoving, and groups of younger workers started the shouting that spread back in waves, increased in volume and tempo, punctuated by hands pounding against the cabs and sides, until both trucks were stopped and surrounded. When people pulled the canvas covering from the first truck and saw the six dead bodies wrapped in polyethylene sheets, the shouting diminished in a fast chain-reaction. Complete silence came within ten seconds.

Slowly, reverently, the first blackened body was lifted by young workers, held high over their heads, passed along to dozens of waiting hands. Seeing each body passed back, naked in the plastic sheets, burned beyond recognition, women began crying, wailing, then screaming hysterically: *"Que paso matados por la compañía! Asesinos! Asesinos!"* From that moment, control was impossible. Led by a twenty-three-year-old laborer named José Portales, more than a dozen young workers scrambled up the sides of the truck, grabbed the three guards from all sides, punched, kicked, wrestled the rifles away, began shooting in the air as they threw the men into the crowd. The thirteen burn victims were rushed off the other truck, the guards jumped, beaten, clubbed, thrown from the truck, then kicked, trampled, spat on. Five policemen on horseback arrived at the height of the melee, plunged into the crowd, swinging clubs indiscriminately; men grabbed at them, hung on to their arms, were carried along as the skittish horses began moving in circles. Two horses reared and bucked, threw the officers, galloped away wildly; the other three men were pulled from their saddles, jumped on, hit with rifle butts, stomped by everyone who could get close.

Jackie and Victor moved along the very edge of the crowd. Carlos watched from the veranda of El Corsario; when he saw the police being trampled, he reached behind his back, slid his hand up under the loose sport shirt, sucked in his stomach, gripped the Luger at the tip of the handle, moved it slowly around to the front. Nilo, standing in the doorway, observed that maneuver as impassively as the action in the street. Kassem and Marquez watched from the porch of La

Paloma Dulce. *"Verrückte Hunde,"* Marquez told himself. *"Bolschevisten."*

José Portales climbed atop the cab of the first truck, rifle in hand, fired two shots in the air, getting the crowd's attention, then shouted in rapid Spanish: "Where are the schools, hospitals and housing we were promised!" A roar of agreement, then silence. "We have *nothing!*" Sweating, holding the rifle up, Portales waited for the roar to soften, then: "And we will have nothing until we show them the power of the *people!*"

In the explosion of shouts and screams, one of the young workers ripped a five-gallon tank of reserve gas from the side of the truck, handed it up to Portales, who began splashing it over the cab and flatbed. He climbed down, ran to the second truck, yanked off the reserve tank, sloshed gas over the length of the vehicle. Lighted matchbooks were thrown. The rear truck ignited first, flames sweeping rapidly; after several attempts, the second one burst into flames with a sudden impact that sent people running. Heavy black smoke billowed straight, then drifted west. Seeing, hearing, smelling, feeling the intensity of the fires, the younger workers lost all sense of fear, followed Portales to an open fruit stand, grabbed anything that was round, began bombarding a single, large, horizontal poster on the wall of a store facing the square. At first, the hard impacts sounded like isolated gunshots; then, quickly, like a machine gun. It was a poster with two rows of four identical photographs each, all of President Ignacio Lopez Guitierrez. In fifteen seconds, the man was unrecognizable.

* * *

HQ 1-21 1646
LARTIGUE MAN DIR PORVENIR ROBERTO DEL RIOS LOCATED VALPARASIO. ETA 0615 REPEAT 0615 VIA DC-3 CHARTER. WILLIAM WHITE LOCATED PUNTA ARENAS. ETA 0630 REPEAT 0630 VIA OWN HELICOPTER. BUDGET PARAMETERS FLEXIBLE TO DEGREE OF DANGER PROBABILITY AND FUNCTIONAL VALUE. ADVISE SOONEST. END.   —WEBBER.

* * *

At six o'clock that evening, all regularly scheduled radio programs aired in southern Chile were preceded by a special announcement, taped earlier in the capital. Although introduced as "A message from President Ignacio Lopez Guitierrez," the voice was that of presidential press secretary Emilio Alvarado:

"Subversion and terrorism by extremists acting in contempt of the government requires that we impose a high concentration of repressive violence in reply. This violence will be exercised with the prudence of men who know their duties."

* * *

Most of the families in Porvenir attended the single voodoo ceremony held that evening at the home of the deceased worker who had the largest house. The structure was located in the slum section near the river and accommodated a maximum of only fifty people, so the various *houngans* and *mambos* arranged for each family to pass through, pay their respects, view several minutes of the torchlit dances, and wait outside for the candlelight procession to the graveyard. On the floor around the central post, the only *vevers* were the flour-drawn symbols of Baron Samedi, the god of death and guardian of the graves: the outlines of six black crosses, the pickax and shovel of the gravediggers, the skull and crossbones, plus six small wooden dolls, hand-carved and painted as undertakers in tuxedos, top hats,

"Sorcerer" star Roy Scheider as Jackie Scanlon.

The "nitro" drivers of Porvenir.... Roy Scheider as Jackie Scanlon.

Bruno Cremer as Victor Manzon.

Amidou as Kassem.

Francisco Rabal as Nilo.

A bomb, planted by Kassem and other Arab terrorists, explodes in a Jerusalem bank.

Kassem (center, in dark shirt) escapes from the police by mingling with a crowd of angry Israelis.

A police officer examines the bloody body of one of Jackie Scanlon's gang, killed during a post-robbery chase.

Wounded, Jackie stumbles away from the death scene.

Learning that a prominent mobster has ordered a "hit" on him, Jackie enlists the aid of a friend to get him out of the country.

Parisian banker Victor Manzon receives a watch as a gift from his loving wife.

In the dismal South American village of Porvenir, Jackie visits the grimy barber shop.

Nilo, a cold-blooded assassin, arrives in Porvenir and begins the search for his target.

Victor Manzon dreams of the lost joys of Paris and tries to accept the bleak reality of the present.

assem, in despair, considers the prospect of a life of back-breaking bor in Porvenir.

The German Marquez (Karl John) and the Arab Kassem share their anti-Zionist views.

Don Carlos (Frederich V. Ledebur) runs the sleazy Cafe El Corsario in Porvenir.

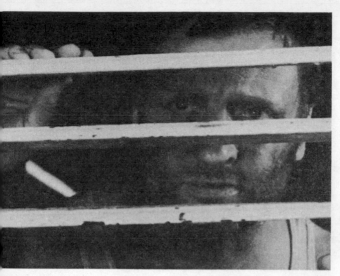

ctor peers out at the miserable world of Porvenir and longs for escape.

ssem broods—there seems no hope that he will ever leave the hell in ich he finds himself.

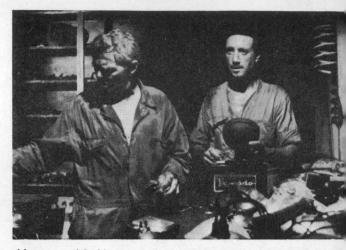

Marquez and Jackie go over their equipment, preparing for the suicidally dangerous mission in the "nitro" trucks.

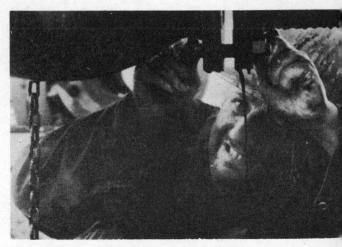

Victor tightens a loose nut on his truck, knowing that even a minor carelessness may mean death.

Kassem, the engineer Corlette (Ramon Bieri), and munitions expert Del Rios (Chico Martinez) begin to load the volatile cases of nitroglycerine into the trucks.

A grim conference before the loaded trucks take to the dangerous, rutted road.

Corlette looks on as Jackie and Kassem study a map showing the route they will take on their perilous journey.

Dawn: the trucks set out.

Revolutionary guerillas attack the nitro-loaded truck driven by Jackie and Nilo.

Nilo kills a guerilla.

Terrified but determined, Jackie hangs on to the wheel and prays....

...that Nilo will be able to guide him across the sagging, storm-battered bridge.

and white gloves. The offering was a single pig.

In the slaughterhouse nearby, two *houngans*, assisted by the professional butcher, were completing the preparation of the bodies. They worked by the light of wood fires in the rectangular room where cows were slaughtered, and went about their tasks swiftly and silently. Drums could be heard from the ceremony just down the alley. Because of the very real fear that loved ones would be turned into zombies, families practiced various measures to prevent revival of the deceased. Of all voodoo practitioners, the *tonton macoute* were the most feared, for their object was to affect the soul, called the *gros bon ange*, or its coexistent, the *'ti bon ange*, sometimes called the zombie. After selecting a victim, the *tonton macoute* would ride to the individual's home at night, seated backward, facing the horse's tail. By placing his mouth to a crack in the door, he would suck out the occupant's soul, then seal it in a bottle. The victim would die several days later, due to any natural or accidental cause. As soon as the body was buried, the sorcerer would go to the graveyard, under cover of darkness, dig up the body, and pass the bottle under its nose. The zombie was then easily led away, a mechanical member of the living dead, without intelligence, emotions or free will, to become a servant of the sorcerer, exploited, overworked, treated severely, given the poorest food, and never fed salt, which would return its will power.

Although there was no way of telling whether any deceased individual had been a victim of such sorcery, families took a wide range of precautions to prevent the creation of zombies, including beheading, dismemberment, vivisection, and firing bullets into the brain. Cremation was forbidden. Since the body could not be revived if the sorcerer called and received no reply, the mouth was often sewn up. Bodies were sometimes buried face down, with the mouth securely wired shut. Despite the country's strict law that required burial within twenty-four hours, bodies were frequently left to decompose in locked rooms; occasionally, an individual would be propped up in a chair before a table filled with his or her favorite food and drink, all to deceive the sorcerer.

In the case of the six dead workers, four of the faces had been burned beyond recognition, and two of the four were mutilated. By mutual consent, the families decided that all six heads would be severed, for maximum protection, the skin removed, the skulls cleaned out, scrubbed in boiling water, then carried to the graveyard by the widows, before each was placed in the casket with its body.

The ceremonial dancing ended at eleven o'clock, and more than five hundred townspeople gathered in the main street near the slaughterhouse, each holding a long, lighted candle. All wore black; most women wore mantillas and carried protective charms—fish bones, goat horns, parrot beaks, alligator teeth, eggshells—to be buried with the men. When the bell from the graveyard was heard, tolling slowly, the *houngans* and *mambos* led the long procession up the dark street, followed by the group of young widows, each holding a skull, then the pallbearers with simple pine caskets, then the children, relatives, friends, fellow workers. It was a solemn march, and slow, a sea of shimmering yellow flames filling the street, revealing faces in opalescent patterns of light and shadow, painting dappled reflections across mud and water, and the voices held primitive emotion: women crying childlike, strangled, hopeless incantations, pleading for mercy from the primordial god of death, progressing toward the unseen bell.

* * *

The barred windows in the rear of the police station cast thin yellow rectangles across the cement courtyard near the stables. Five stallions, still skittish from the experiences of the afternoon, moved restlessly in the stalls, uttered low sounds. High humidity accentuated the smell of manure. In the small harness room, two lanterns illuminated the face of a twenty-three-year-old man standing against the wall. He wore a battered hat and held a cigarette in the side of his mouth; smoke curled up toward his right eye, making him blink rapidly. A black man stood by the open door, lean face sweating in the heat, wearing a black hat, blood-red necktie, black shirt and trousers. He nodded to a sturdy, stocky officer with a trim mustache, who approached the young man, snapped the cigarette from his mouth, yanked his hat off, pulled a black hood over his head. A single fly buzzed loudly around the ceiling, batted against the window slats.

In the abrupt darkness, *We have nothing!* José Portales was crying at last, *And we will have nothing* but silently, shaking, sweating, *until we show them* somehow shocked at the reality, the proximity, *the power of people!* feeling the ropes cut into his wrists, *Liars!* feeling blood rush to his head, *Conjurers!* feeling his heart pounding, *Betrayers!* faster, louder, harder, *Why couldn't I kill the illusion,* and something like a ringing sensation *destroy it, tear it out of my mind and heart?*

140

in his ears, louder, higher, stronger, *The contradictions would've been explained*, then broken by the sharp click of the .45 slide pulled back *the questions answered*, to compress the recoil spring *the torment ended* and cock the hammer *But it's over now* As the slide clicked forward, *Finally, finally, it's over*, the breechblock stripped the cartridge *there's an end to it*, from the magazine lips, and chambered it, *a finish, at last* and the extractor in the face of the breechblock *The truth is known*, snapped into the extracting groove *the lie is dead*, of the cartridge case *the reality is found*, The grip safety was squeezed, *the illusion is lost* releasing the automatic disconnector *Or is it?* Pressure on the trigger *For the final irony*, freed the hammer from the sear, *the one I suspected all along*, the hammer rocked forward on its axis *is that I simply cannot live* to strike the firing pin, *cannot live* and the pin snapped forward *cannot live* to strike and fire the cartridge *with that truth.*

* * *

When he heard the shot from the stable, followed by very loud whinnying of the horses, the sad-eyed officer in the steel-rimmed glasses took a sip of Coke and glanced at his watch. He turned on the radio, moved the dial to the all-night music station that would carry the news at midnight. Four minutes later, the news was preceded by a special announcement from President Ignacio Lopez Guitierrez, taped earlier in the capital, and read in a flat monotone by presidential press secretary Emilio Alvarado:

"As a result of the patriotism and courage of the workers of Porvenir, in cooperation with the civil and military authority in that area, the consequences of the unfortunate accident at the COREPET oil field were reduced to a minimum. There were a few minor injuries, but no deaths were reported."

9

At 6:45 Saturday morning, Billy White's U.S. Army-surplus helicopter lifted off the mud runway in Porvenir with Corlette and an industrial engineer named Bobby Del Ríos, and headed northwest for Poza Rica. It was the same model White had flown in Vietnam eleven years before, a Bell HH-1H, powered by a T53-L-13B engine with 1,400 sph thrust, and a maximum speed of 138. Although most of its vital parts had been replaced in the seven years he'd spent as a freelance pilot in Punta Arenas, it was a dependable craft, and the only one to be had within a radius of some three hundred miles. White, a tall, skinny, thirty-four-year-old with a shake in his voice, kept it full throttle all the way, and the three men had to shout every word to be heard. Del Ríos, twenty-seven, muscular, dark-haired, with a thick mustache, headed a small Valparaiso firm that sold heavy fire-extinguishing equipment.

143

He'd gained something of a reputation among oilmen as an expert in fighting well fires.

"In San Felipe," he-shouted, "we had to pump mud into a well. Hell of a job getting it up there. They cleared a strip, but the weather was too bad to fly."

Corlette nodded, pointed down. "There's a piece of the road."

"You got an airstrip at the well?"

"No. Ground's too rough for any heavy equipment." He indicated a section of the road in the distance, winding up a valley toward the mountains. "That's the way in."

White increased his altitude gradually as they approached the mountains. The peaks were hidden in clouds. Visibility was zero when they passed the peaks, then gave way to lush green jungle for many miles. They could see the helicopter's tiny shadow rippling across the crowns of the trees.

"At least you got a lot of water in this country," Del Ríos shouted. "I had a fire in Bolivia last year with no water. We had to *truck* it in."

They became silent as they caught glimpses of the canyons and bizarre landscape of the Culo del Diablo in the distance. The buttes and mesas threw long shadows in the early morning. When they passed over the twisting canyons, the wind currents changed abruptly, the pitch of the rotor volume increased, straining, and the ride got rough. The currents leveled out when they cleared the final ridge, and they saw the huge column of black smoke. From that altitude, it seemed stationary, like a black stalagmite jutting into the sky. And, given the almost extraterrestrial condition of the landscape they'd just passed, it didn't seem out of place, somehow, until they were two miles closer and could see the tower of flame beneath smoke that shot over a thousand feet before billowing. The mushroom was so thick that its shadow blacked out miles of jungle to the west.

White lost altitude gradually, then circled the geyser. The area around it was saturated with foam and mud, littered with debris, and teams of workers were still spraying the base with four long high-pressure hoses, as they had done in shifts throughout the previous day and night. You could hear the constant roar above the rotor noise and vibrations, and the smell was bitterly pungent, irritating the nose and eyes. After circling six times, and asking White to pause in midair several times, Del Ríos leaned toward Corlette; his eyes were watering.

"Well, I've seen worse!" he yelled. "Let's clear away all that junk and blow her out!"

* * *

The magazine housing the company's supply of nitroglycerin was located a mile behind the refinery in Porvenir. The area had once served as a machinery yard, when the pipeline was just starting, and it had been abandoned for over a year then; the jungle had long since begun its process of reclamation. At 10:05 that morning, Corlette, Del Ríos, and a COREPET guard used large machetes to hack their way through to the magazine. They were sweating heavily and out of breath when they reached the little shed. The rotted wooden door had a faded red PELIGRO sign, but it wasn't locked. Del Ríos removed a stick from the latch; the door stuck, then creaked as it opened. Inside, the air was very hot and dry. Shafts of sunlight revealed six stacks of wooden cases, piled five to a stack, covered with heavy dust and mildew.

Del Ríos entered slowly, touched one of the cases, studied the underside of the lid. He reached his left hand back, spoke softly: "Machete."

The guard, who wore an old steel helmet, handed it to him, then stepped forward for a better view.

"Stay back." Del Ríos stood at the side of the stack to allow maximum light, carefully pried up the end slat, then the others. Using slow, deliberate movements, he unwrapped the heavy brown paper, pulled open the yellowed polyethylene bag, removed one of the fat brown sticks, examined it in the dim light. He peeled off one end, rubbed his thumb over the white powder; it crumbled away like sugar.

"This stuff is too dry to fart." He tossed the stick to Corlette, turned to the guard. "When did you last turn these cases?"

"I don't remember."

Del Ríos glanced into the polyethylene bag, inserted his hand slowly. The deeper he went, the more cautiously he moved. He felt something at the bottom, froze, began to withdraw his hand with extreme care, wrist rigid, fingers straight. Corlette and the guard moved back in the silence, staring at his wet fingertips.

Keeping his forearm, wrist and hand in the same vertical position, he stepped softly, slowly, to the door, crouched and swiveled to his right in the same graceful motion, snapping his wrist, flinging the drops to the concrete. The series of tiny explosions threw sparks, sounded like shots from a cap gun.

He took a deep breath as he looked at his fingers, stood up, continued to speak softly. "That stuff's been sitting the better part of a year. It's worthless."

147

"What do you mean?" Corlette asked.

"When it sits for a long time without being turned, that liquid nitro seeps out of the sticks and into the bag. If you give those cases *any* kind of a bump, it'll blow."

Corlette thought about it, wiped the sweat from his forehead. "If it were up there, could you use it?"

"I suppose we could boom-load a little bit at a time, yes. How the hell you—"

"That's not your problem. We'll get it up there."

* * *

On Corlette's instructions, Billy White experimented with various methods of shock-mounting dummy cases. Del Ríos believed the fire could be blown out with one to three cases. At 12:30, while Del Ríos and White filled two large canvas bags with sand and sawdust, Corlette attached a bottle of water, half filled, to the dash of the cockpit to determine exactly how serious the vibrations would be. The bags of sand and sawdust were placed on the two rear seats. White positioned the cases on the bags, and Del Ríos wired them to the seats, then attached cross-wires to the rear and sides of the cockpit. The cases looked quite secure.

White took Del Ríos up for a half-hour of straight-line flying toward Poza Rica. After the first ten minutes, the water in the dash-mounted bottle settled down a bit, swaying, but when they gained altitude, as they'd have to do over the mountains, the air currents became unpredictable, bouncing the 10,500-pound chopper, and the water splashed crazily. White tried it at maximum speed, but the vibrations were far too bad.

"No way," Del Ríos told him. "Let's head back."

White nodded, began his turn. "We could try a pallet."

"How far under?"

"Thirty, maybe forty feet."

Del Ríos considered it. "What about lift-off and landing?"

"I got a winch cable. We'd lower it gradually."

By 1:15, they had the cases and bags mounted on a three-by-four-foot wooden pallet. Heavy guide wires were attached to the four corners of the pallet, then wired together in pyramidal form, with the apex attached to the winch cable hook. Before starting the engine, White operated the winch manually, raising the load a foot off the runway. When he lifted off slowly, he shifted the winch to automatic, began lowering the pallet at an altitude of twenty feet. Del Ríos kept his window open, leaned out as far as the seat belt would allow, watched as the pallet moved down, swaying. The rotor noise was extremely loud. At an altitude of only two thousand feet, the wind was so strong he had to shield his eyes to keep them open.

White tapped him on the back, pointed to a compartment under the dash. "Binoculars!"

Del Ríos couldn't hear, but opened the compartment, spotted the binoculars, grabbed them and leaned out again. The eye cups were effective shields, and he focused on the cases quickly; they continued to move down slowly without a sign of vibration. White locked the winch at thirty feet, then concentrated on gaining altitude. When he reached six thousand feet, the air currents began changing abruptly and the wind in the cockpit was strong and cold; he was wearing an old white sailor's cap with the brim turned down, and had to hold it on with his left hand. At seven thousand feet, the chopper began to bounce and rattle; Del Ríos saw the pallet sway sideways in the wind, then swivel to the left, hold for a while before turning back. At eight thousand feet, just below a thick cloud bank, the ride became very rough; the pallet was swiveling back and forth at 180-degree angles.

Del Ríos leaned in, closed the window. "How much cable you got?"

"In all? Seventy-five feet."

"Lower it to sixty feet."

"What's it doing?"

"Swiveling like hell."

White leveled at eight thousand feet, began lowering the pallet very gradually. When it reached sixty feet, Del Ríos opened the window, placed the binoculars to his eyes before leaning out. The pallet had moved far back under the cockpit. He released his seat belt, leaned out as far as he dared. When he focused, the pallet was being buffeted from side to side and the swiveling motion had gained considerable momentum.

White turned back at 1:55, leveled at four thousand feet, pulled in the cable swiftly. They reached the runway at 2:10. An old Lockheed Electra turboprop was parked by the airport shack, boarding burn victims for the flight to Bonao. Corlette was there, supervising. Del Ríos got out dejectedly, walked to the shack for a soft drink. White was starting to disassemble the pallet mount when he saw Corlette walk toward him with two Cokes.

He handed him the bottle. "What do you think?"

White walked with him toward the shack. "The major problem is the vibration. This thing is like a damned egg beater. No matter how we shock-mount something, it'll still have a severe lateral vibration."

"I thought maybe you could—uh—sling-load it on a pallet."

"About twenty feet down, there'd be no vibration, but the problem's turbulence. You might move it half a mile that way, but not two hundred. I've never had a flight around here without some turbulence in it."

Corlette stopped, took a deep breath, exhaled audibly. What he really wanted was a simple, direct answer, something he never seemed to get from anybody. "What're you saying, Billy?"

"Not with a chopper. There's no way."

"I'll double the amount if you can think of a way."

"It's not the money, Mr. Corlette. Nobody's going to get into a chopper with that shit. You need a suicide jockey."

* * *

HQ 1-22 1439
LARTIGUE MAN DIR PORVENIR
BONAO GENERAL HOSPITAL
BURN UNIT STANDING BY. SEVEN

REPEAT SEVEN EMERGENCY VE-
HICLES ASSIGNED TO AIRPORT.

EFFECTIVE IMMEDIATELY CMA
ALL NON-MANAGEMENT REFIN-
ERY EMPLOYEES LAID OFF UNTIL
NORMAL OPERATIONS RESUMED.
NON-MANAGEMENT   PAYROLL
STOPPED EFFECTIVE 1700 FRI-
DAY.   RETAIN   MAINTENANCE
CREW ONLY.

INFORM CORLETTE CMA EFFEC-
TIVE IMMEDIATELY CMA HE IS
INCLUDED   UNDER   MANAGE-
MENT EMERGENCY PERSONAL
ACCIDENT INSURANCE POLICY
CMA COVERING ACCIDENTAL
DEATH CMA DISMEMBERMENT
CMA PERMANENT TOTAL DIS-
ABILITY. REIMBURSEMENT FOR
MEDICAL EXPENSES NOT PRO-
VIDED.

POLICY PROVIDES COVERAGE IN
EVENT OF INJURY OR DEATH
CAUSED BY ACCIDENT AND SUS-
TAINED ANYWHERE IN WORLD
CMA WHILE RIDING AS PASSEN-
GER IN CMA BOARDING OR
ALIGHTING FROM CMA OR BE-

ING STRUCK BY ANY AIR CMA
LAND OR SEA CONVEYANCE CMA
OR WHILE OPERATING ANY COM-
PANY VEHICLE DURING EMER-
GENCY CONDITIONS.

ADVISE SUBSEQUENT ACTIONS
SOONEST. END.   —WEBBER.

❊   ❊   ❊

At 3:15, the market square was crowded
and noisy as Corlette and Zayas were driven
slowly up the main street in the back of a
COREPET pickup truck. They stood just behind the cab, and Zayas held a battery-pow-
ered bullhorn. He switched it on, blew into
it, testing, then began addressing the crowd
in Spanish: "The company has an important
announcement. An important announcement
for the people of Porvenir, from Charles
Corlette, chief of operations at the oil field."
The truck bounced slowly through the puddles. A few doors and windows opened, and
some women and children stepped outside,
squinting in the sun, shielding their eyes,
many dressed in underwear. As the truck
passed La Paloma Dulce, Zayas repeated the
same introduction, but more forcefully. Slowly, the street below the market began to fill

with people; dogs started yelping, running toward the truck. Corlette glanced at the faces of people who walked alongside.

Before the truck reached the noisy square, he took the bullhorn, spoke softly: "We regret, very sincerely, the suffering among you that this fire has caused."

As Zayas translated, Corlette glanced at the black hulks of the two burned COREPET trucks in the square, down on their rims in the mud. The crowd was getting bigger, keeping pace on both sides of the truck.

He continued: "We also regret that a few troublemakers used the incident as an occasion to destroy company property."

During the translation, the truck finally stopped in the crowded square, not far from the burned hulks. The townspeople gathered around, listened in silence.

Corlette raised his voice: "We now need experienced truckdrivers. Men who are willing to do a dangerous job."

Jackie maneuvered his way to the front of the crowd. He moved past a family of jungle Indians, glanced at their faces. They were smiling at Zayas's translation, not understanding that any more than the English, but thoroughly enjoying the free entertainment.

"This job *must* be done before we can reopen our gates and bring back full employment to you people."

155

Kassem moved along the edge of the crowd, wearing a cloth headband, staring at Zayas as he translated.

"The men who qualify, they will receive *exceptional wages.*"

There was a pause after the translation, just a beat, then people began shouting questions simultaneously. Victor watched with Carlos and Marquez from the porch of El Corsario. Nilo stood nearby.

Corlette lifted his hands. "*Silencio, por favor, silencio.* Now, many of you know that road. It's very bad." In the translation, Zayas emphasized *Es muy malo.* "Only experienced truckdrivers willing to risk their lives can do it. No one else should apply."

The crowd was silent through the translation, and Corlette studied faces, trying to gauge the reaction.

"The company will pay *eight thousand pesos* to each driver."

Before Zayas had finished translating, dozens of workers started walking away, realizing how much danger must be involved if the company offered that kind of money. Some left with loud parting shots: "*Que no somos locos! Quieren más muertos por la compañía!*" A chain-reaction of loud shouting followed, hundreds of voices trying to be heard above the noise.

Corlette's voice was grizzled as he shouted them down with the bullhorn: *"Silencio! Silencio! Silencio, por favor!* Four men—with enough *guts!*—can save Poza Rica and your village!"

*　*　*

The nine volunteers were a very mixed lot, with foreigners dominating, and Corlette took them to the motor pool at the refinery, where he selected a heavy, old, ten-gear truck for the driving tests. Before leaving, he mounted a small bottle, half filled with water, on top of the dashboard, and told the men that the movement of the liquid would be his most important consideration in making the decisions. The men piled in back and he drove them out to the cemetery road for the tests, as it was one of the very worst and most isolated in the area, with only one small village nearby. He had their names listed alphabetically, and gave the tests in that order: Castelli, Dominguez, Jair, Kassem, Kefalos, Marquez, Martínez, Nilo, Serrano. As each man took his test, the others rode in back.

When Castelli shifted up through the medium range of gears along a straightaway, he was confident to the point of cockiness. A recent arrival in town, the twenty-eight-year-old Italian was built like an athlete and spoke English fairly well. The bottle of water remained reasonably stable until he started up the first hill and had to shift down three. Sweating, cursing, he pulled and pushed the stick, heard the gears grind. The truck lurched half a dozen times, jogged the water into a wild dance. He barely made it up the hill, kept on fighting the gears as he started down, confidence completely lost.

"Stop at the bottom of the hill," Corlette told him coldly.

His voice shook. "I need to know the machine!"

"*Pull! Over!*"

Jackie had Corlette eating out of his hand from the first minute: He pulled the release knob of the air brake, changed the gear level from the medium to the low-range transfer case, quickly scanned the dash for the air-pressure indicator, then threw the switch that unlocked the front anchors. Corlette glanced at him, frowned.

Jackie threw it in gear, started smoothly. "It'll steer better on the dirt with the front anchors unlocked."

Corlette watched him slide effortlessly through the whole range of gears, up and down hills, around curves, eyes moving from road to side-view mirror to bottle to road to rear-view mirror, never looking at the stick as he shifted. He held the big wheel in the nine and two o'clock positions, grip firm but not tight, controlled by the fingertips. When he turned left, he didn't invert his right hand to pull, kept it flat, feeding wheel to the left hand, sliding the right on and off in circular, graceful movements; right turns were equally smooth and rhythmic, as if the wheel was an extension of his body.

Corlette made a note on his clipboard. "Teamster?"

Jackie nodded, then lied easily. "Grey-hound."

Jair, a young black, drove with typical Brazilian abandon, roaring around the curves, flooring it to get enough speed for the hills, then double-clutching on the way down, happily oblivious to the bottle of water. When Corlette shouted something he couldn't hear, he turned, smiled broadly, and hit an enormous bump that nearly threw them both out of the cab.

Kassem handled the lower gears well, then shifted to the higher range on a relatively smooth section of road. As they rounded a curve near the village, he was hitting forty-five, and Corlette's right foot slammed on the floor automatically when he saw three kids playing in the middle of the road not fifteen feet away. Kassem didn't touch the brake. The children scattered, screaming, and the left edge of the bumper missed one of them by inches.

"You crazy *bastard!*" Corlette shouted.

Kassem calmly glanced at the water in the bottle.

Breathing rapidly, heart pounding, Corlette realized only too well that cold, instantaneous decisions of that kind were perfect for the job, made a note of it on the clipboard.

Next on the list, Kefalos, a middle-aged Greek, was so shaken by the near-miss of the child that he relinquished his turn, asked to take the test last.

At fifty-seven, Marquez's reactions weren't as fast as the four previous drivers, but his self-assurance was obvious as he turned the truck around on Corlette's orders, maneuvering the heavy vehicle back and forth on the narrow road, taking his time. When he neared the spot where the children had been playing, he shifted down, took the curve well, then alternated his attention between the road, bottle and mirrors. Corlette waited to see how he handled the big bump that Jair hit. Even driving toward the sun, which was low then, making him squint, Marquez spotted the bump fifty yards ahead, down-shifted immediately, brought the truck to an almost total stop as he inched over it, then accelerated smoothly.

Mario Martínez was a forty-four-year-old local whose driving abilities were well-known to Corlette. He lacked initiative, but he was steady, dependable under ordinary circumstances, and would do if the others turned out to be as bad as Castelli and Jair. Corlette let him go through the motions for half a mile, asked him to pull over, thanked him.

The real surprise was Nilo. Judging by his clothes and unassuming manner, Corlette suspected that he'd never driven a heavy truck in his life. The old man sat carefully in the high seat and examined the series of levers that controlled the lower range of gears and different axles. Before starting the engine, he made a dry-run through the changes. Corlette braced himself, sat rigidly as Nilo turned on the key, revved the engine, eased off the air brake and pulled ahead into the strong sun. His eyes were wide behind the dark glasses, moving from road to bottle, and he only glanced at the stick for the first four shifts. Corlette relaxed gradually, somewhat puzzled. A man didn't learn to drive a rig like that by studying the gears. Obviously, he'd had experience, probably many years ago, and all the dozens of little subtleties were coming back to him. His thin hands looked very pale against the big wheel as he made a sharp right, then left, swinging the old machine around from lock to lock. When he climbed the hill Castelli had such difficulty with, he down-shifted quite well. After another mile of wrestling with the sheer size of the wheel, he began to tire, coughing in short spasms. Corlette had to admire the man's nerve, but that was it. He'd never last. He'd be exhausted after fifty miles.

With concentration and caution, Victor managed to catch the rhythms of the truck's complicated shifting patterns, and Corlette felt a strong sense of confidence in the way he handled himself. He wasn't in the same league with Jackie, but he had all the moves, excellent reflexes, adequate hand-eye co-ordination.

"You've had experience," Corlette said.

"Yes."

"Where?"

Victor glanced at the bottle, down-shifted for a long curve. "Armored cars in Algeria." He said it thoughtfully, frowning.

Finally, the frail Kefalos sat behind the wheel, breathing hard, face and shirt soaked with sweat. Before starting, he studied each of the gauges with utmost concern, twice moved the shift through the lower range of gears. Corlette, apprehensive, glancing at his watch, was just about to tell him to forget it, when the man started the engine. He checked the gear lever for the last time, depressed the clutch, blinked at the gauges, clearly afraid to make the final moves that would set the vehicle in motion.

Corlette braced hard. *"Vamos."*

Kefalos gunned the motor loudly, far above the needed RPMs, kept it going as he released the air brake, then abruptly let up on the clutch. The rear tires squealed, the truck lurched forward, hurling the men in the back to the floorboards. Instantly, Kefalos hit the brake, tossing the men forward. Eight voices shouted curses.

Corlette reached over, turned off the key.

Kefalos sank back on the seat. *"No me siento bien."*

* * *

By 6:30 that afternoon, the oil storage tank closest to the administration building had turned a deep orange against the mountains, and its cylindrical shadow extended beyond the fence and into the yard where the men waited. Outside the front gate, a small crowd of the curious had gathered quietly, taking the sun's valediction with an air of reverence, fingers gripping the rusted fence, faces patterned by dark quadrangles of chain link. Jackie leaned against the fender of the dust-covered truck they'd used for the test, looked at the people outside the fence, then concentrated on Nilo, across the yard, who was using a handkerchief to wipe the sweatband of his hat. His bald pate glistened, and his white suit was wrinkled and a bit dusty. Each of the men remained separate from the others, with the exception of Kassem and Marquez.

At 6:35, one of the double doors of the front entrance opened quickly, banged back against the wall, and Zayas came out, holding a clipboard. He waited for the men to walk over to him, but they didn't.

He spoke loudly: "Serrano . . . Dominguez . . . Marquez . . . Kassem . . . wait here. You others can go."

Zayas went back inside, closed the door. Jackie lit a cigarette, glanced at Victor. Kassem and Marquez watched Nilo as he put on his hat, adjusted his sunglasses, and followed the rejected men toward the gate. They walked slowly, single-file, their shadows sharp and long on the dirt.

* * *

Seen from the refinery at dusk, the massive western mountains were solid black against a deep red burn that softened in the upper atmosphere, coloring the bases of long, flat, stratiform clouds that hung motionless. The land colors took intensely vivid shades, became iridescent, as if before rain. Victor watched from the open louvered window of the recreation hall, to the north of the administration building, and remembered what Agrippa told him: that at the split second when the sun disappeared behind the mountains, there was a strange green flash sometimes. He'd watched carefully for the first few weeks, but he hadn't seen it.

His attention was distracted by a loud electric whir. At the little bar in the corner, Corlette had turned on the blender, mixing the daiquiris. Rather than negotiate with all four men, he'd asked for a spokesman, and Victor had been the unanimous choice. Jackie, Kassem and Marquez had been driven back to town. They were all scheduled to meet at 6:30 next morning at the motor pool to prepare the two trucks.

While the blender whirred, Victor studied the map. The noise reverberated around the large, sparsely furnished room, but it was a familiar sound, reminding him of the kitchen in his home on Avenue Foch. For an instant, he visualized Blanche in one of her favorite St. Laurent dresses. He shook his head to obliterate that image, but others kept coming. *No one is "just" anything.* Blanche and Lydia leaving the Pre-Catalan, laughing in the cold December sun. *In Mexico, they kept telling us about the lobster in Veracruz.* Walking to their cars in the parking lot. *He said* we *took the risk,* we *must pay the consequences.* Their footsteps making soft, slow, crunching sounds on the gravel. *You've got to speak to him again.* The strong smell of decaying leaves from the Bois de Boulogne. *I can't do it.* The top of Pascal's Porsche Targa holding soft reflections of the trees. *Within seconds, I would make a simple gesture.* The large rear window of the Porsche *that would remove her from the face of the earth* was shattered and streaked red. *Whose gesture would remove me?*

Corlette switched off the blender. The whir of the blades softened, dropped low, stopped. Victor heard the pleasant, heavy-liquid sound as the daiquiris were poured. Corlette walked slowly around the bar, passed the Ping-Pong table and the jukebox. When he handed Victor his glass and sat down, his face had the severe lines of a bookkeeper. He continued the conversation of five minutes ago, as if only a few seconds had elapsed:

"The ride was pretty smooth at about fifteen miles an hour."

Victor nodded. "Twenty hours."

"One man can sleep while the other drives."

"No one will sleep."

Corlette sipped his drink, looked at the map. "When you head toward Poza Rica, there's a rough climb, and when you clear the top, watch for this piece of washboard." He pointed to the area. "Our drivers take it at forty-five miles an hour. You want to write that down?"

"I won't forget." Victor took a drink.

Corlette leaned forward, tapped his finger on the map. "Here, you come down into the rain forest, and there's this detour to the bridge. The road in the forest is usually okay, unless there's been a lot of rain. There's a big climb here, 'the grind'—eight thousand feet. From there, the road is—fairly decent all the way to the well." He paused, sipped, glanced at Victor. "I've driven it at least a hundred times. It's not good, I won't bullshit you." He studied the map again.

"We've decided to decline."

Corlette glanced up quickly.

"We have probably less than a fifty percent chance of success. Your offer is too low. It's clear that both trucks are carrying identical loads because only one is expected to make it."

Corlette took a drink, stared at the map. He took another, longer drink, stood up, walked slowly to the bar, then glanced back. "No decent limes in this country. We have to use grapefruit."

Victor nodded, remained silent.

"Serrano, you deserve better than to rot here. Forget the money for a minute. Our company has pull with the government. I can swing legal residence. You could live anywhere, even in the capital, without looking over your shoulder."

"I appreciate your offer. I'll add it to our demands."

"I'm talking about *you*, Serrano."

"I speak for the others as well. I can't drive two trucks alone."

Corlette took a deep breath, studied his drink. "Five thousand dollars apiece."

"Double that, and your offer of legal residence would be acceptable."

"I'm not authorized to go that high."

"Not authorized to spend twenty thousand to save twenty million?"

Corlette shrugged. "There're five hundred men in that town. I'll get other drivers."

"Only one of the locals volunteered. Even

the police won't anger the spirits of the road by hauling explosives over the Paso al Infierno. The stupid are also superstitious. I'm afraid you're stuck with us." Victor lifted his glass. "This is excellent. Cheers."

10

Seen from a distance, they both resembled extinct land reptiles of the Mesozoic age, Cretaceous period, relatively large, perhaps as tall as ten feet, maybe twenty feet long, cold-blooded, lung-breathing vertebrates, ranking higher than amphibians, lower than birds or mammals; not erect-walking tyrannosaurs, but heavy, scaled creatures, possibly mutations, their bony plates and horny shells light gray in the first vestiges of morning light, black legs crouching, eyes huge, glassy, dazed almost, dimly aware of several anthropoids crawling around their bodies. Seen from a closer angle, it would be obvious to students of the species that both apparitions, although remarkable in themselves, barely resembled their proud progenitors. Yet the physical discrepancies were not inherited; they had clearly been inflicted, often viciously, over a lifespan of some thirty-five years, in a violent struggle for survival.

And, somehow, they had survived. That is, the essence of them had survived, through some curious accident.

Seen from the window of Charles Corlette's office in the administration building, they were frightening. For a number of reasons, primarily emotional. Frightening because he remembered when they arrived, more than four years ago; was it possible he'd been down here four full years of his life and then some, spending half his time at the field, half at the refinery? Frightening because he could vividly remember others of their species when he was young, when he was with the U.S. Army Engineers in Europe, more than thirty years ago. And, finally, frightening because they looked so ravaged now, compared to what they had been: Diesel-powered, ten-wheeled, heavy-duty U.S. Army Transports, manufactured during World War II by General Motors at one of ten plants in Flint, Michigan. General Motors, which converted its assembly lines to war production, not only in the U.S., but in—and for—Nazi Germany as well. General Motors, which, after the war, almost unbelievably, had the balls to sue the U.S. Government for wartime damages to its German facilities.

Corlette leaned out the window, watched

the four men working with his motor pool crew, climbing all over the old rigs. The shack that served as a garage for the motor pool was loaded with used parts from all kinds of trucks, including G.M. military transports that had been completely disassembled when the diesel engines gave out, and those parts were being used to maximum advantage now. He'd given them one day to get both trucks in shape and load the nitro. They'd leave at dawn on Monday.

Jackie's experience with trucks proved extremely valuable, particularly his knowledge of diesel engines. He took charge of the operation from the beginning, with no objections from the others. Kassem's first assignments were to remove the doors from both trucks, find eight of the largest vertical side-view mirrors in the garage, then attach them to the doorframes and front fenders at angles that would allow both driver and passenger to see the rear wheels and the road immediately in front of them. Victor was instructed to remove and inspect all twenty tires, replace the most worn, realign, and reduce the air pressure uniformly by ten pounds. Marquez, who had some experience in welding, was told to collect ten of the best headlights he could find, test them, construct two five-foot horizontal platforms, weld five lights to each, attach them to the roof of each cab, and use extension wires to connect them to the electrical systems. The three men in the motor pool had the job of attaching two electrically operated winches, with 100-foot steel cables, to the front frames of the trucks, directly under the bumpers, then mounting gearboxes on the cab floors next to the transmission gearshifts, and wiring them.

The engines were Jackie's prime concern, and he studied the ignition systems first. Unlike conventional internal combustion engines that ignited fuel by spark, the diesels had compression-ignition systems in which a spray of oil, introduced into air compressed by the pistons to a heat of 1,000° F., ignites at a virtually constant temperature to provide the power stroke. After removing the crankcase on both trucks, Jackie observed the actions of each crankshaft and piston, confirmed that both engines had four-stroke cycles rather than the more common two-stroke, then studied the cycles carefully. During the intake stroke, as the piston lowered in its cylinder, the intake valve opened, admitting a mixture of oil and air, and the exhaust valve was closed. In the compression stroke, both valves were closed as the piston moved back up, compressing the air.

In the ignition and power stroke, the valves remained closed as the compression-ignited oil forced the piston down. Finally, in the exhaust stroke, the intake valve remained closed, and the exhaust valve opened as the piston moved up, expelling the heated air. On one of the engines, the rod connecting the piston to the crankshaft had been bent, only slightly, but enough to interrupt the shaft's elliptical orbit by a fraction of an inch, placing strain on one side of the piston. The rod had to be replaced. In addition, the intake and exhaust valves on both engines were too worn for efficient performance; he replaced them with valves that were also used, but in marginally better condition. After he finished changing the oil, replacing the filter, and cleaning the tungsten-tipped distributor points in both trucks, there was a definite change in the sound of the engines.

About 10:30, Bobby Del Ríos arrived in a pickup truck loaded with bags of sand and sawdust. He poured a layer of sand over the bed of each truck, spread it evenly to a thickness of four inches, then emptied the bags of sawdust over the sand, spread it into a layer six inches thick. Before noon, he left for the machinery yard with a crew of six workers supplied by Corlette, and all the equipment needed to clear the area in front of the explosives magazine, set up a generator, string lights, remove the magazine's front wall, and rig a rope-and-pulley system for loading the cases.

Shortly after 1:30, Nilo walked casually into the motor pool area, looking somewhat different in a short-sleeved sport shirt, dark trousers, and no hat, although he still wore his dark glasses. He kept his distance, observed for several hours as the men climbed over the trucks, mounted the platform with headlights atop each cab, attached a long row of fog lights to the front bumpers, tested the winches and cables, replaced tires and shock absorbers, painted the word PELIGRO in bright red letters on both sides of the trucks. The men were really too busy to pay much attention to him, but his presence made them nervous, particularly Kassem, who gave him periodic cold stares until he finally left.

As Jackie was tightening the screws for the shovel rack on the passenger side of the truck that was nearest the garage, he saw part of a word on the frame just above the running board; years ago, it hadn't quite been covered by the gray company paint sprayed over the regulation Army brown. It looked like the typical hand-lettered nickname that GI drivers always gave their ve-hicles, brushed on with an amateur flourish, a forerunner to modern graffiti. He could see only five dark red letters to the right: CERER. But, when he ran his fingers over the left side of the word, he felt the other three. He looked at the thing from various angles, then felt the hidden letters again, to be sure.

Marquez stood in the door of the garage, watching him. He rolled out one of the big replacement tires Victor had selected, stopped when he reached Jackie. Since English was his worst language, he pointed to the letters. *"Meinen?"*

Jackie looked at him, frowned.

"Vouloir dire?"

"No comprendo."

"Significado?"

Jackie looked in the man's eyes, wondering if he had a sense of humor. He held up a forefinger, then put his hand to his forehead, as if searching his limited vocabulary for the most approximate translation. He was just about to say *Muerte*, when he thought of a better name. Placing his hand on Marquez's shoulder, he said the word softly, almost reverently: *"Tormento."*

❋   ❋   ❋

HQ 1-23 1723
LARTIGUE MAN DIR PORVENIR
RE YOUR QUESTIONS HOSPITAL-
IZED BURN VICTIMS CLN WHEN
CMA AS RESULT OF-INJURY ON
JOB CMA ANY NON-MANAGEMENT
EMPLOYEE IS TOTALLY AND PER-
MANENTLY DISABLED AND PRE-
VENTED FROM ENGAGING IN
EVERY DUTY OF HIS OCCUPA-
TION FOR A PERIOD OF AT LEAST
12 REPEAT 12 CONSECUTIVE
MONTHS CMA AFTER WHICH HE
IS PREVENTED FROM ENGAGING
IN ANY SUBSTANTIALLY GAIN-
FUL OCCUPATION OR EMPLOY-
MENT FOR REMAINDER OF HIS
LIFE CMA COREPET WILL PAY
AMOUNTS SHOWN UNDER
SCHEDULE OF INDEMNITIES CMA
SUBJECT TO IDENTICAL LIABIL-
ITY LIMITS PROVIDED IN CLASS
IX BASIC LIFE INSURANCE FOR
MANAGEMENT AND SPECIALIST
EMPLOYEES.

EMPHASIZE NON-MANAGEMENT
VOLUNTEERS SELECTED TRANS-
PORT EXTINGUISHING EQUIP-
MENT CANNOT REPEAT CANNOT
RECEIVE COVERAGE UNDER

SAME SCHEDULE CMA AS ALL NON-MANAGEMENT PERSONNEL OFFICIALLY TERMINATED EFFECTIVE 1700 CMA 1-21 CMA EXCEPTION MAINTENANCE ONLY. VOLUNTEERS CLASSIFIED PAID CONSULTANTS. END. —WEBBER.

* * *

It was dusk when the two trucks moved along the forest road toward the old construction machinery yard, and the branches of the palm trees, heavy with leaves, arched across both sides of the dirt road and grew into each other, forming a long green tunnel in the headlight shafts. Birds, frightened by the lights and roar of the diesel engines, seemed trapped in the tunnel, flying erratically, searching, and at least a dozen small animals stood in the road as if paralyzed, blinded by the lights, jumping to the side only in the last few seconds. Marquez drove the lead truck, Sorcerer, with Kassem at his side; Jackie had refused to ride in that truck. The one he drove, with Victor studying his moves, also had a nickname, Lazaro, painted across the hood. All four men had worked more than twelve hours on the trucks, taking only a short break for lunch. They were exhausted, but Corlette insisted that they load the nitroglycerin immediately after din-

178

ner, so they could be ready to leave for Poza Rica at dawn.

When the trucks arrived, Del Ríos was still working with the six-man crew, and the area around the magazine was brightly lighted, cleared of undergrowth. The generator hummed very loudly above a steady chorus of frogs. They'd removed the corrugated front wall and were busy stringing lights inside. Kassem and Victor got out and guided the trucks to the magazine, picking up remaining fragments of rusted junk. As Sorcerer was the lead truck, it would be loaded first. Marquez turned it around, backed up slowly, stopped on command, locked the air brakes.

Del Ríos took charge of the loading operation. He had all the equipment he needed, went to work quickly and efficiently, giving instructions to the others. Each truck would carry three cases of nitro, arranged in a triangle. In Sorcerer, two cases would be positioned near the cab, one near the tailgate, all equidistant. Each case would be tightly crosswired to the sides, to the back near the cab, and to one another. The rope-and-pulley system had been rigged, anchored securely to the back of the truck and the rear frame of the magazine, producing a clothesline effect.

When Del Ríos finished tying the first case,

Jackie took his position far back in the truck
near the cab; Victor climbed up on the edge
of the tailgate; Marquez would operate the
ropes. Kassem slid his fingers carefully down
the sides of the case, took a firm grip, then
turned to Marquez and nodded. The pulleys
squeaked as the case moved slowly toward
Victor, who was braced and waiting.

* * *

The next morning, Monday, January 24,
when Victor passed Agrippa's shrine and
glanced at his Lucian Piccard in the predawn light, it was 5:52, and he knew he'd
have plenty of time to meet Corlette and the
others outside El Corsario at exactly six.
He'd been worried that he wouldn't have
enough time to concentrate on the letter to
Blanche, but he'd awakened at 4:45, and
he'd written it with a clear head. It was a
good letter, and an honest one, and it af-
forded hope. If the drive was successful, she
could eventually meet him in Santiago, if she
wanted to, and they could continue, if she
wanted to. He hadn't pulled any punches,
because he owed her the whole truth. If the
drive failed, if he didn't get to Poza Rica,
he'd either be back where he started, or he'd
be dead. He told her that he thought about
her constantly, that he was deeply sorry and

disgusted for what he'd done, and that he would always love her. He asked for her understanding. Passing through the kitchen, he held on to the letter in the deep right-hand pocket of his jacket; he'd ask Corlette to mail it for him.

From the veranda, the rows of corrugated shacks extending down to the river were merely diminishing silhouettes, but he could see long red streaks in the cirrostratus clouds above the eastern Andes, and the familiar puddles in the mud were just starting to take shades of orange. In the absence of any breeze, the smell of rotting fruit and vegetables was particularly strong. The only sound at first was the steady, soothing monotony of frogs and insects, punctuated by faraway barks after a while, then finally broken by the breathless, hysterical shrieks of the first pig being killed in the cement courtyard of the slaughterhouse. The cries lasted just twenty seconds, ended in a noise that sounded like a sharp retch.

Before the next one was killed, Victor heard the hum of a distant truck. In less than thirty seconds, he could see its head-lights swing into the main street, engine groaning, the old three-quarter-ton flatbed that would take them back to the explosives magazine where the trucks were loaded and ready. As it picked up speed, bouncing, splashing, springs squeaking, three men appeared from one of the side streets, then several others, workers who had watched from the gate of the administration building the previous afternoon, wanting to see them off now. Shortly after the truck passed La Paloma Dulce, Victor recognized the figures of Jackie and Kassem starting to walk toward him.

The truck made a wide, mud-splattering U-turn in front of El Corsario, pulled up to the veranda. When the motor stopped, the squeals of another pig were heard. Corlette stepped out of the passenger side, holding a large thermos and some plastic cups. Victor walked over to him. They exchanged nods, didn't speak. Corlette unscrewed the top of the thermos, removed the cork, handed Victor one of the cups. As he poured, steam drifted from the black coffee, and Victor thought he saw the man's hand shaking, although it was hard to tell in that light.

Five or six workers gathered around, watched in silence. Jackie and Kassem arrived, footsteps making soft sucking noises. Corlette gave them plastic cups, then climbed in the cab, opened the glove compartment, handed out a box containing cubes of sugar and small packets of cream. Kassem scooped up a handful of sugar cubes, stuffed most of them in his jacket pocket, dropped five into his coffee, handed the box back. Jackie blew on his coffee, walked to the rear of the truck, eased himself up on the back, watched the clouds brighten over the mountains. He wore his only hat, a dark, narrow-brimmed fedora, and a dark-red jacket.

Corlette took a folder from the seat of the cab, opened it, handed a copy of the equipment list to Victor, went back to give a copy to Jackie. Kassem stood off by himself, moving his cup of coffee from side to side, trying to cool it.

Jackie studied the list. "Only one machete?"

Corlette shrugged. "How many would you like?"

"We might have to put half the jungle underneath our wheels to get through the mud."

Corlette turned to the driver. *"Hay machete en este camión?"*

"Sí, hay dos." He went to get them.

"There should be two," Corlette said.

Jackie went back to the list. "Condensers, points, fuel, filters, crowbars, tape, wire, rags . . . where's the rest of this cable?"

"It's over there in the car." Corlette glanced up and down the street impatiently. "Where the hell is the German?" He motioned to the driver. *"Toca el claxon."*

The driver blew the horn in two long blasts.

As Victor glanced at the driver, he saw Agrippa standing on the veranda. In the soft orange light, her long hair looked like it had just been washed, parted carefully in the middle, and she wore a simple black dress, in mourning for the dead workers. It was her best dress, the only one that revealed her slim figure. She held Victor's gaze for a few seconds, then came down the steps and walked toward him, barefoot in the mud.

Corlette saw her, spoke abruptly. *"Qúe quiere?"*

She hesitated, glanced down, and spoke rapidly, just above a whisper. *"Tengo algo para el Señor Serrano."*

He looked at Victor. "She's got something for you."

Embarrassed, Agrippa kept her eyes averted as she stepped forward, took Victor's right hand, pressed her gift into it. She closed his fingers over the charm, not wanting anyone to see, and her eyes were wet when she looked up at him. *"Para su buena fortuna, Señor Serrano."*

Before Victor could say a word, she turned and walked very quickly toward the veranda, dark hair bouncing, feet making soft slapping sounds, tiny drops of mud rising to sprinkle the backs of her legs and the hem of her black dress. Victor opened his fingers just a fraction, looked, closed them again, put his hand in his jacket pocket.

"What is it?" Jackie asked.

Victor just winked at him.

Corlette glanced at his watch, motioned to the driver again. *"Toca el claxon."*

Agrippa walked swiftly up the veranda steps and hurried to the door. The horn blared twice. As she entered, she passed Nilo, on his way out. He touched the brim of his hat, walked to the edge of the steps, looked toward the mountains, where the sun was just beginning to appear. Victor shot a glance at Jackie, then Kassem. They'd both seen him.

Kassem slurped his coffee slowly, stared at Nilo, who leaned against the wooden pillar, adjusted his dark glasses. Victor was about to light a cigarette when he saw Kassem's expression and posture freeze, cup poised inches from his lips, as if receiving a signal that only he could see or hear or sense. He remained in that position for a full five seconds, then threw his cup to the side, spraying a semicircle of coffee that caught the sun for an instant, and bolted into a sprint up the street toward the deserted market square. Kicking back a rhythmic shower of mud all the way, he ran past the two burned-out trucks, then turned left into the first side street and disappeared.

Marquez lived in an old wooden cottage three doors in from the square. It was distinct by its cleanliness, small and simply furnished, painted brown, with yellow louvered doors and windows, and a gray clapboard roof. When Kassem ran up on the little front porch, sweating, out of breath, yelling the man's name, he grabbed the door handle, turned it both ways, pushing, then slammed his weight against it, before remembering that it opened outward. It wasn't locked. He screamed the name this time, yanked the door open, ran directly ahead to the bedroom. The louvers of the window to the east were slightly open, emitting horizontal bars of orange-yellow sunlight that played across the foot of the bed, rippling to the contours of a faded blue quilt, neatly folded. The fair-haired, fair-skinned, fifty-seven-year-old man was on his back, face in shadow, muscular arms outside the top-sheet, by his sides, in an attitude of untroubled repose, as if the strenuous labor of the previous evening had exhausted him beyond even unconscious anxiety of what would come next. Kassem came closer, whispered his name, then repeated it aloud, but softly. A single fly buzzed loudly around the ceiling, batted against the window slats. As his eyes adjusted, Kassem could see that the man's face and arms seemed abnormally pale, particularly the face, against the under-sheet that appeared dark. He said the name again, blinked, leaned forward, and his voice made a strangled sound when his hand touched the soaked sheet. His palm shook when he looked at it. He didn't examine the man's throat, because the blood there and on the mouth had already coagulated to a thick brown coating.

Kassem wiped his palm on the side of his jeans, whispered an oath in Arabic, turned, felt his legs shake as he walked through to the front door. Outside, he broke into a run again, repeating the oath to himself over and over. Turning right on the main street, he took out his switchblade, clicked it open, ran at top speed toward the distant white figure that became a bouncing, undulating blur in the first shafts of sunlight.

Victor and Jackie had their backs turned, leaning over the equipment list on the bed of the truck, but Nilo saw Kassem coming from the start, walked calmly down the veranda steps, and stood ready, arms at his sides. When Victor and Jackie finally saw him, they ran to head him off, but didn't quite make it. Nilo waited until Kassem was almost on top of him before pivoting, like a matador performing a skillful veronica, then threw a hard right to the side of his face. Kassem went sprawling in the mud. As he scrambled up, Victor grabbed him, Jackie wrestled the knife away.

"*Murderer!*" he screamed. "*Zionist!* I'll *kill* you!"

Corlette ran over. "What happened? What *happened!*"

"This Jew dog cut his throat!"

Corlette swung around to the driver. "*Vete avisar la policía.*"

"No police," Jackie said softly.

Corlette yelled at the driver: "*Vete por la policía!*"

"*Hold it!*" Jackie shouted, then spoke quickly, softly: "We just lost a driver. We need another one."

Corlette frowned, started to reply, then glanced at Nilo. In the silence, the shrill monotonous tones of a single cicada sounded very loud, as if it was in their midst. One by one, involuntarily, the men looked at Nilo. He stood straight, touched the frame of his dark glasses, smiled calmly. His complexion was distinctly copper in the soft yellow light and his breathing was measured, just slightly audible. Before he spoke, it occurred to Corlette that he'd never actually heard the old man's voice. He hadn't said a word even during the driving test.

"When the money's up," Nilo said with a strong Spanish accent, "I'm as good as any of you."

11

It took five minutes for the big diesel engine to warm up, and Jackie used the time to check gauges, lights and mirrors. Nilo sat next to him, smoking calmly, studying the map. They were scheduled to leave first; Victor and Kassem would wait fifteen minutes to permit a separation of at least several miles. Jackie tapped against the air pressure gauge, waiting for it to come up, and glanced at the rifle mounted on the passenger side of the dash. Corlette had equipped both cabs with a Winchester 30-30 lever-action carbine, and Jackie was thoroughly familiar with the weapon. He'd once owned the same rifle, Model 94, and practiced fairly regularly at the West Side Rifle & Pistol Range, 20 West 20th Street, in Manhattan. It was dependable, extremely accurate, and the lever action was fast and easy. Although the recoil was hard, it weighed only six and a half pounds, had an overall length of just thirty-seven and three-quarter inches, a twenty-inch barrel, and the tubular magazine held six rounds.

The odometers in both trucks had been set at zero, because the maps indicated danger spots in terms of distance traveled. As the air-pressure gauge moved up and steadied, Jackie rummaged around in the glove compartment, found a small piece of chalk, wrote "218" on the dash next to the odometer. He revved the engine, released the air brake. After easing it into low and feeling the clutch engage, Jackie took a deep breath, stepped lightly on the accelerator. Corlette, Victor and Kassem watched in silence as Lazaro's big tires moved over the ruts in the yard. It was for real now, finally, and after all the preparation, anxiety and tension that kept building, Jackie felt a definite sense of release in the simple fact of motion. He also experienced the strong confidence that always came whenever he got behind a wheel.

When they approached the main street, Nilo cleared his throat. "Where you from?"

Jackie didn't even glance at him. "Listen, Pancho, I been clocking you every second since you got into this town. If you're going to pick your nose on this truck, you better clear it with me first. Because if you don't, I'm taking you and this nitro right into a ditch."

191

They made the turn, and Jackie shifted up two gears as they passed the slaughterhouse, then down one when they reached the riverbank and moved through the shallow water. The current was swift, but the riverbed was relatively flat; Jackie had driven Spider's truck through it numerous times. After clearing the opposite bank, he shifted up, kept it at about eighteen miles an hour on the straight sections.

*　*　*

At 6:30, the sun was already very strong in the machinery yard. Sorcerer, still beaded with moisture, threw a long shadow that went halfway up the side wall of the magazine, made a zigzag pattern in the corrugated grooves.

Corlette checked his watch, looked up at Victor in the passenger side. "They've had fifteen minutes."

"Yes." Victor climbed down slowly, reached in the pocket of his jacket, spoke quietly. "I have a letter. I wonder . . . if you would post it for me."

Corlette took the small white envelope, glanced at the address. "Paris. That could take a month."

"Yes." He looked in the man's eyes. "Just keep it for me."

"I'll take care of it."

Kassem started the engine, revved it immediately, anxious to get going. Victor shook Corlette's hand, nodded his thanks, climbed in.

        ❊   ❊   ❊

Nilo fingered the wooden doll in his pocket. The sky had clouded over and it became very hot in the cab, despite the missing doors. For the first half hour, the drive was so monotonous that Jackie had to keep reminding himself to hold his speed constant at about eighteen. There were long stretches of road flanked by tall palms and tangle, mile after mile. After a while, he began to feel claustrophobic, looked forward to the next bend in the distance, and then, same thing: narrow brown road and walls of dismal green. Occasionally, when he encountered chuckholes filled with chalky water, it was almost a pleasure to shift down and go to work again. Nilo kept glancing back at the nitro through the cab's rear window.

"Why'd you hit the German?"

Nilo looked at him, smiled. "I flipped a coin."

"Kraut lost, huh?"

"No. You did."

For an instant, Jackie went cold. It was

the quiet, calm way he said it more than anything else.

Nilo smiled again. "But I'm partial to Americans."

The road ran parallel to the pipeline as they passed to the left of a small Indian village. They were starting to climb a little then, and the branches of the trees were draped with long, graceful Spanish moss, a welcome change. Then the road began to wind, very gradually, and when Jackie saw an Indian family about a hundred yards ahead, he didn't give it much thought. They all turned, walked to the left side, stood there and watched. Jackie glanced up from the road as he came closer, then had to look again to be sure. It was the same Indian family he'd seen in town, the young father and mother, the little boy and girl, except that they were practically naked in the heat. He tried to keep his eyes on the road, but, unaccountably, their presence disturbed him. Then the father moved forward.

He smiled up at Jackie with the same delighted, innocent expression he'd had in town, bright white teeth filed straight across, eyes sparkling with the unexpected excitement of the strange-looking truck. Jackie returned his attention to the road, then realized that the Indian was jogging alongside. Nilo leaned forward, watched, sat back and lit a cigarette. They both made an attempt to consciously ignore him, thinking that would discourage him. But it didn't. He ran joyously along, began laughing, pounding his chest, then shouted words that couldn't be heard over the motor. From the corner of his eye, Jackie watched the man make little leaps as he ran. After a minute or so, the truck had to slow for a large hole. Instead of slowing to a walk, the Indian ran up on the pipeline, arms spread, as if walking a tightrope, laughing, then dancing, even doing pirouettes, Jackie eased over the hole, shifted up again, and the Indian stayed right with him. His laugh had the genuine excitement of a child.

But the Indian wasn't making fun of them. That's what hurt. In the young man's mind, it was a magical contest with a huge mechanical monster that had invaded his domain. It unnerved Jackie, because the happy simplicity of the Indian's life seemed to make a mockery of his own fear, his work, his desperation. Fragments of questions flashed into his mind, questions he simply couldn't allow himself to ask. He felt more alone in those few minutes than he'd felt in years. The Indian kept pace, sprinted ahead just a little, let the truck catch up to him, laughing, playing his marvelous new game.

Finally, when he began to run in front of

the truck, Jackie had all he could stand. First he blasted the horn; when that didn't do any good, he leaned out and shouted; *"Get outa there!"*

Nilo leaned out the oother side. *"Cuidado! Cuidado!"*

"Come on, move it! Get the hell outa there!"

With that, the Indian became even more excited. He leaped twice, very high, shouted something, broke into a fit of laughter. The road looked reasonably smooth all the way to the next bend, so Jackie took a calculated risk, slammed the shift quickly, accelerated to about twenty-one. He hit a small bump almost immediately, cursed himself, but didn't shift down. The Indian scrambled to the side of the road then, running very hard, sweating, still smiling. Before they reached the bend, he tripped on some undergrowth, stumbled, and fell hard. Jackie glanced in the rear-view mirror. The Indian was sitting at the side of the road, head thrown back, laughing hysterically.

After another couple of miles, they climbed along a narrow stretch of road that followed the natural curve of a hillside. At an arroyo made by a small stream bed, the road took a very sharp bend. A section that had been washed away was supported by wooden construction that resembled a bridge. The gap was spanned by about fifty yards of heavy logs, buttressed by a series of long wooden poles driven into the side of the hill. Jackie slowed, shifted to compound low, negotiated the turn with extreme care. In the fender-mounted mirror, he watched the logs strain under the weight of the rear tires. The logs looked almost white in the sun, dry and brittle. He heard them squeak, then splinter slightly, inching apart. It was the same all the way across. On the other side, Jackie tilted his hat back, took a deep breath, glanced at Nilo. He couldn't see the man's eyes behind the dark glasses, but sweat ran down the side of his face.

* * *

When Sorcerer reached the same construction about fifteen minutes later, Victor stopped, walked out to examine the span with Kassem. Most of the logs in the track sections were splintered, some were cracked, others were separated by as much as two inches. They inspected all fifty yards, returned to the truck, stood there, squinting in the glare. Kassem was mad as hell.

"I'll guide you," Victor told him.

"*You* drive and *I* guide *you!* Okay?"

Victor kept his voice low. "Get in the truck."

Cursing, Kassem jumped in the cab, shifted to compound low. He drove with deliberate, measured motions, hugging the side of the hill as much as possible, as Victor walked backward, giving hand signals. After only twenty yards, the logs in front began to spread more, groaning and splintering. Both front tires started sliding into the crevices. Kassem stopped, accelerated slightly. The tires merely went in deeper, spinning. He made one final attempt, but the wheels were in so deep that the whole front of the cab was tilted.

Knowing he'd have to back out, he jumped down, examined the front wheels with Victor, then checked the back to see how much room he had. There was no guardrail, and, at that point in the turn, the left set of double rear tires was approximately seven feet from the edge. When he eased it into reverse and touched the accelerator, the rear tires squealed. He applied more pressure. Same result. The third time, the truck lurched back suddenly; Kassem hit the brake fast, glanced at the fender-mounted mirror. The left set of tires was actually over the edge, still spinning.

Victor waved his arm. "Come on!"

"*No!*"

"Come on!"

Shaking, Kassem shifted back to compound low, obeyed Victor's hand signal to turn a fraction to the right, moved ahead, bumped over three logs, turned straight gradually.

* * *

Lazaro's odometer read twenty-three miles when the road changed from dirt to gravel, and the climb became steep. Visibility was excellent, but the humidity was increasing, and the air smelled of rain. Jackie leaned out of the cab several times, taking the breeze on his face. Nilo had removed his coat.

"Check the map," Jackie told him.

Nilo picked it up, unfolded it on his lap.

Jackie squinted at the odometer again. "We're twenty-three miles out. What've we got?"

Nilo took off his sunglasses, held the map almost at arm's length. "There's some kind of mark at fifty-seven miles."

"That's the washboard." Jackie began to shift down, slowed carefully, pulled over, stopped. He threw it in neutral, locked the emergency air brake. "You drive."

Nilo folded the map, coughed as he climbed out and walked around the cab. Jackie slid over. They were in an area of lush green palms and moss. Even with the motor idling, Jackie could hear streams of water running down the side of the hill to the right. Nilo adjusted the seat forward a notch, checked the outside mirrors, tilted the rear-view mirror down a bit, glanced at the air pressure gauge.

"Keep it around eighteen miles an hour," Jackie said.

He depressed the clutch and eased it into gear before pulling the release knob on the air brake, then moved ahead smoothly, shifting through the lower range of gears. Jackie watched his moves carefully; they weren't exactly fluid or rhythmic, but he obviously knew what he was doing.

About forty-five minutes later, they were still climbing, and the winding road was so smooth that Nilo hadn't had to down-shift even once, kept it almost dead-on eighteen miles an hour. Heat shimmered up from the gravel. It began to get cloudy as they went higher, and a lot more humid. Jackie's eyelids drooped when he looked at the odometer: thirty-five miles. Another twenty-two before the washboard. He planned to take over when it read fifty-five, just to be on the safe side. That would give him another hour or so of rest, and he'd need all he could get. As they wound around one of the long turns, he could see a really beautiful rain forest below; he tried to concentrate on it to keep his eyelids up. When it suddenly hit him that they were descending, it was too late, the up-and-down vibrations had already started. He was wide awake in an instant, seeing the deep, regular bands across the road that defined the washboard.

"Jesus *Christ!*" he shouted. "Get *on* it!"

The bumps became severe so fast that Nilo panicked, down-shifted immediately, the very worst thing he could do.

Jackie lunged over, grabbed the throttle, yanked it out all the way. "*Go*, God damn it! *Faster! Faster!*"

When Nilo heard the engine roar without his foot on the gas, and felt the acceleration, he hit the brake, but Jackie kicked his foot off it.

"I *can't!*" he shouted. "I can't *control* it!"

"Don't *think!* Just do what I tell you! *Clutch!*"

They were bouncing on the seat. He hit the clutch; Jackie moved the shift up one gear. They picked up speed, continued to bounce. "Okay, clutch!" He stomped on it; Jackie went up another gear. More speed, same bounce. "Clutch!" Up another gear. They started to swerve. Nilo strained with the big wheel. More speed. "Clutch!" Up another. When the speedometer reached forty, the bouncing was reduced, but they were swerving badly.

"I can't *hold* it!"

"Clutch!"

He hit it again, Jackie shifted, and the speedometer went up to forty-five. Seconds later, the bouncing was almost under control, but the truck was swerving from one side of the road to the other. Nilo was turning the wheel back and forth with everything he had. Finally, he went for the brake again.

"Don't *touch* that! *Steer* it out! She'll come *out!*"

Jackie didn't have time to spell it out for him, but he got the general idea, remembered some long-ago training he'd had about how to handle a skid on ice. As soon as he began steering in the direction the truck was headed, they started to level off. Not much, but enough. When Jackie was reasonably certain the old man had it under control, he pushed the throttle back in, very slowly, and let him take over. The truck hummed along for a while, still weaving a little and bumping, but they could see the end of the washboard down the road. As they passed over the last of the deeper, regular bars, Nilo began shifting down. It didn't take him long. He slowed it to a crawl, pulled over. Just before he stopped, he forgot to depress the clutch, and the motor began to lug. He banged his foot on the pedal, slammed the shift, hit the brake, threw it in neutral, locked the emergency brake.

They sat back in silence, sweat dripping, breath coming hard. Nilo's arms and legs were shaking. He looked like he'd had a coronary.

"Get out," Jackie said softly.

He climbed down unsteadily, then had to hold on to the fender as he walked around. He looked like a very old man. For some reason, seeing him like that, Jackie felt a lot stronger. He'd been badly shaken, too, but he experienced a strange sense of confidence again as he slid behind the wheel. He grabbed the map from the floor, threw it open, slapped it down against the wheel. Nilo climbed in with an effort, then sat back, stared straight ahead.

"*Kilometers!*" Jackie shouted. "That frog marked this God damn thing in *kilometers!*"

Nilo sat there like a dead man. When he began to cough, softly, he didn't put his fist to his mouth, as he'd always done. He just sat there and coughed, sweating, eyes staring fixedly behind the glasses.

Jackie tossed the map on the dash, put it in gear, revved the engine, pulled the emergency brake, and took off down the incline. Kilometers, he thought. An American engineer with an American company, sending us out in American military transports with

American mileage odometers, then marking the most critical points on the map in kilometers. Then it occurred to him that he was the only American of the four.

At about 8:30, the sky began to darken, investing the trees with vivid but fragile shades of green and brown, the air cooled, and within ten minutes large drops of rain began spattering the windshield. Jackie turned on the wipers and the regular set of headlights; the odometer read thirty-six miles. Corlette had marked a detour route to the river eighty-three kilometers from the start, and he tried to work out what that would be in miles. Whenever he'd driven big rigs on long hauls, he used to figure average mileage, speed and time, to stay alert, but he'd never had to deal in kilometers. All he knew was the fact that one kilometer was approximately sixty-two percent of a mile. He decided to work it roughly. Call it sixty percent. Point sixty times eighty-three. Forty-nine point eight. Call it fifty. About fifty miles from the start. That meant around fourteen miles ahead. At eighteen miles an hour, they'd be there in about forty-five minutes.

The road remained good most of the way down, and the rain wasn't hard, just a steady drizzle. At 9:25, he saw a Y-junction in the distance with a tree in the center. As he came closer, the headlights picked up the figure of a man walking along the left side of the road toward the junction; he wore a wide-brimmed hat, leaned on a cane, and had a pronounced limp. When he passed the man, he began shifting down, stopped about ten feet in front of the tree. A metal arrow that had apparently been nailed to the tree had fallen off. It was sticking in the ground by the trunk, point down. Jackie pulled the emergency brake, shut off the engine, got out, walked up to the tree in the rain. From what he could see in the headlight shafts, the two roads looked almost identical, both gravel, both about the same width. He shook his head, went back for the map.

As he walked out of the headlight beams, he heard the man limping toward him, slowly, cane scraping the gravel. He seemed extremely old. Although his face was shadowed by the wide hat brim, Jackie could see his white beard and the deep wrinkles around his eyes. Nilo got out, walked around, as the man reached the cab.

Jackie nodded, squinting in the rain.

The ancient man just looked at him.

Jackie pointed to the left of the junction. "The road to Poza Rica, *sí*?"

"*El cruce*," he said softly.

Nilo walked up to the man very slowly,

tipped his hat, spoke quietly. *"Por favor, Señor, puede usted decirme dirección?"*

"El cruce."

Nilo nodded. *"Dónde está el desvío a Poza Rica?"*

"Tengo guardián del cruce."

Nilo held the man's gaze for a few seconds, turned to Jackie, spoke confidentially. *"Loco."*

They both got in the truck, and Jackie grabbed the map, held it under the dashboard light. Corlette had just marked "Detour—83," without indicating which road to take. He studied the topography. The road to the left apparently went up along a canyon wall; the other seemed to run through swampland. Both led to the river. He handed Nilo the map without a word, released the brake, pulled ahead to the left, heard a horn blasting in the distance. He stopped, leaned out.

About a quarter of a mile up the road, Sorcerer was blurred in waves of rain, as if moving underwater. The horn blared again; its echoes were distorted in the mountains. Jackie put the brake on, shut off the engine, climbed out slowly. He glanced at the old man by the side of the road, then squinted, held a hand up to shield his eyes, watched the truck approach. It shimmered, melted from side to side, then came back in focus a few seconds at a time. The headlights were dim yellow. Shadows of trees moved quickly over the cab, made flickering patterns. It reminded him of something from a recurring dream, *His face was high up on the dash* an image on the threshold of consciousness *and the top of his head* that gave him a sickening sensation *was locked in the shattered windshield* The old man limped past, *He was trying to say something*, distracting him just momentarily, *but his mouth was pressed against the dash* and the vague image that almost surfaced was lost.

Sorcerer crunched along the gravel, gears shifting, stopped slowly to the right of the junction. Kassem was driving.

Victor got out, holding the map. "That's the wrong road."

Jackie walked over to him, pointed left. "I think this road's better for us, because it's *higher*."

Victor nodded to the right. "We take this one."

"No, you don't understand." He looked at the map, traced his finger along the road. "This—this road's too low, it goes through the *swamp*. There's too much *mud*."

"Can you read a map?" Victor asked calmly. "We have no information on that road."

"You're full of *shit!* You take that road!"

Victor grabbed him by the front of the jacket, but his voice remained calm. "We follow the map."

12

VICTOR RECOGNIZED THE CLOUDS that drifted east toward the mountains, the kind of dense, tall white towers that meteorologists identified as cumulonimbus, a class indicative of thunderstorm conditions; clouds that ranged in vertical length from three thousand to twenty thousand feet; clouds that took strange, solid shapes, except for the tops which appeared fibrous because of the presence of ice crystals. As he waited at the Y-junction with Kassem, giving Jackie and Nilo the required fifteen-minute head start along the road to the right, he continued to feel oddly calm. The rain was diminishing, but he knew it was only temporary. The sound of its soft spray was broken only by distant birds, not singing, but calling in long, lingering cries, almost plaintive, sensing the real storm's proximity. He watched the dark figure of the old man with the wide-brimmed hat as he moved along the straight road to the left, becoming smaller and smaller, bent over slightly, taking short, slow, limping steps, leaning on his cane. He walked in the middle of the road, dwarfed by the trees. The oncoming storm obviously held no anxiety for him.

When Victor walked to the front of the cab and lit a cigarette, he smelled decay in the breeze, a damp, sharp odor of rotting leaves. Kassem's footsteps made soft, slow, crunching sounds on the gravel *Pascal got in the car*, as he walked to the front, *closed the door, opened the window*, glanced at the massive layer of clouds, *then sat motionless*, holding his dirty cloth headband *staring straight ahead*. He looked very young in that light.

"Where's your home?" Victor asked softly.

Kassem sat on the bumper. "I was born in Jerusalem. I grew up in—in Lebanon. In a refugee camp."

"I've never been to the Middle East. But I know North Africa." He nodded to himself. "Quite well."

"You were there during the French aggression?"

Victor took a drag on the cigarette, inhaled, released the smoke as he talked. "I was in Algeria. In Oran . . . I was nearly killed. My armored car was hit by a shell. My friend . . . it took his head away. I re-

210

member cleaning his brains . . . off the inside of the turret. But, when it happened, I felt nothing. It was just a duty. I cleaned him up . . . and it meant nothing to me."

Kassem stood up. "And now?"

He drew a deep breath, exhaled. "I'm no longer political."

"What is your job?"

"I was . . . in investment banking."

"Very political."

"Only indirectly."

Kassem laughed softly. "I think very directly."

* * *

The lightning was silent when it illuminated the river for the first time, and Jackie counted the seconds between the flash and the thunder, almost automatically, as he'd always done. Six seconds later, it was relatively loud, a series of crackles first, then the heavy bursts, like explosions, followed by long, low rumbles, softening as it echoed in the mountains. He'd seen enough of the bridge in that single flash to know it would be difficult to cross. The river was already roaring through the canyon in a muddy, debris-filled current that was getting swifter by the minute. The final stretch of road to the bridge had a steep grade, slick with mud in the rain, and even Jackie's skill couldn't prevent the truck from sliding into a sharp lean as it came down. It leveled as he drove to the edge and stopped.

He got out and walked to the bridge. In the rain, he had trouble focusing on it, and the span was partially obscured by a fine mist rising from the river, looking like fog. It was a temporary bridge, its wooden tracks suspended from two steel cables passing over small support towers, then anchored at the ends. He couldn't see the other end clearly, but he calculated the span at between seventy and one hundred feet. The original bridge was to the far left, a dark silhouette.

He stood still in the rain, spoke to himself, and, for the first time, his voice held a trace of hysteria. "It's the wrong road. *This is the wrong road!*"

When he walked out on the bridge, squinting, holding the steel cable, he could feel it sway, and water was starting to rush across the middle of the tracks. He walked back carefully through the mist, stepped off, then ran back to Nilo's side of the truck.

But Nilo wasn't there. He was already running back along the road toward the grade, kicking back mud, white suit glistening.

"Where the hell're you going!" Jackie took off after him, sprinting at top speed, blinded by the rain, feeling a burst of energy so

212

strong that he knew his body was out of control. He heard his throat make a guttural sound when he tackled the old man, leaping, springing on the white suit, then biting, clawing as they both sprawled, tumbling over and over in the mud. His throat kept making the sound as he scrambled up. When he finally spoke, tasting mud, his voice had the high, hysterical, primitive anger of an animal:

"We're gonna cross that bridge! And you're gonna guide me! 'Cause I can't do it alone!"

Nilo sat up, nodded, rain spattering his face. He picked up his glasses and hat, struggled to his feet, held his back as he walked to the bridge.

A flash of lightning startled Jackie when he climbed into the cab. He counted, silently, watching Nilo move slowly to the edge of the bridge. Seven seconds. No crackle this time, just three discontinuous blasts, so loud that Nilo actually hunched over in automatic reflex. Then the long rumbles, the echoes.

As Jackie drove forward, inching it, Nilo squinted without his glasses, stepping backward, squatting, giving hand signals, suit already drenched and looking white again in the downpour, water streaming from the brim of his hat. He used both hands, motioning left, left, straight, more left, straight, watched the front tires finally move onto the wooden tracks. Immediately, the weight submerged the tracks a little, then more as the cab's rear tires moved on. Jackie alternated his glances between Nilo and the fender-mounted mirrors, moving inch by inch, stopping, checking. Finally, all ten tires in position, he gripped the wheel so hard his knuckles showed white, accelerated with infinite care. Nilo moved backward on his haunches, held the cable with his left hand, motioned with the right. Even with the roar of the current and rain drumming on the roof, Jackie could hear a series of sharp cracks as the track boards split. At midpoint, the bridge increased its weaving movement with the growing force of the current. When the front tires began sliding off the tracks, Nilo grabbed the support cables, pulled against the current, actually tipped the bridge with strength that surprised Jackie. The front tires slid back a fraction. Nilo braced himself, used his weight to rock the bridge against the current. Inch by inch, the tires moved back to the center of the tracks, and Nilo waved Jackie ahead angrily. In the mirror, Jackie saw that the rear tires were half submerged at that point, but the rest of the crossing was a slight upward climb, and he knew the worst was over when he gave it a bit more power and felt the traction hold.

Nilo began backing up and sitting, giving hand signals that were more angry than precise. A very brief flash of lightning made him wince; he held the boards with both hands, braced in anticipation of the discharges that came four seconds later, then went back to work.

When they reached the end, Nilo stood, stumbled to the side. Jackie gunned it off the bridge, and the sound and motion were luxurious to him. He slammed on the brakes, waited for Nilo to climb in. Keeping it in compound low, he drove swiftly up the grade, turned into the gravel road, stopped and looked down at the bridge in the gray light. A large section of the middle was completely submerged then, and the current continued to rage, picking up momentum with the storm. Nilo, catching his breath, didn't bother to look back.

"Tough luck, Serrano." Jackie pulled ahead, shifted up, accelerated, jerked his head unnaturally as he scanned the road, the mirrors, the gauges; began a rhythmic squeezing of the steering wheel, squirming in his seat. His voice was shrill, out of breath: "You'll never cross that bridge. You guys've *had* it. That's twenty thousand, that's twenty thousand *apiece*! You hear me?" He shifted up again, whispered, "Twenty thousand, twenty thousand," then began the monologue again, louder, with more conviction: "Yeah, those guys've *bought* it. They're never gonna make that *bridge*, I'll tell you that. They've *had* it! We're sitting on double *shares!* Twenty *thousand! Twenty thousand apiece!* That's a lot of money, I'll tell you that!"

❋　❋　❋

Only eight minutes later, when Victor eased Sorcerer down the steep, mud-slick grade, sagging, then leveling as it reached the edge and stopped, approximately fifty feet of the bridge was submerged, and, along the middle, tree branches and brush were jammed against the steel cable on the upstream side. Victor and Kassem got out, walked down slowly, studied the weaving, bobbing cables and fast current, listened to the constant metallic groans of the support pilings. From the bank, the wooden tracks were only visible for a distance of some seven feet before vanishing into the foam and mist. The steel cables above water gave the only tangible indication that the bridge actually extended all the way across.

Kassem waded out to the middle of the span, where the current was almost up to his knees, removed several large branches that were entangled in the cables, tossed them downstream. Victor got in the cab, shifted to compound low, drove close to the tracks to begin positioning the wheels. Kassem came back, rain pelting his face.

Victor leaned way out. "Stay close!"

Kassem waved, nodded, stood directly in front of the bumper. He crouched to study the front wheels, stood to give hand signals.

It required eleven minutes to reach the middle of the span, where the swaying was very bad. The huge wheels were half submerged. Instead of using the mirrors, Victor leaned far out, strained to see them; they were barely turning. When a sudden increase in the current caused the bridge to undulate, Victor grabbed the wheel hard, felt the truck begin to yaw. In less than a minute, the current seemed to subside. They inched forward again. Brief flashes of lightning didn't seem to affect either man; the thunder was distant. A large log rolled swiftly toward the bridge, jammed in the pilings, causing the rear wheels to rise almost out of the water, then begin to slip sideways on the tracks. Victor accelerated carefully. The rear wheels started to spin. Kassem rushed to the back, gripped the cable, watched the tires spin as they continued the slow slide.

"*No!*" he yelled. "*Reverse!*"

Victor slammed it into reverse, inched back, felt the traction return, eased it to compound low. Kassem watched, immobile except for the motion of the bridge. When the wheels finally cleared the slight elevation and returned to deeper water, he slogged ahead, studied the position of the front wheels, signaled for forward movement. The truck was well past midpoint, traction adequate, wheels moving into progressively more shallow water, when the current became stronger again, muddy water surging with branches, palm leaves, brush, and, as the bridge swayed, Kassem held on to the fenders, glanced upstream, and saw the tree coming.

It was a whole tree, roots, trunk, branches, enormous and heavy, tumbling at them so fast that Kassem only had time for one short scream before it slammed into the bridge with tremendous impact, knocking him into the river. Victor caught a glimpse of it before a tangle of branches tore into the cab, jammed into his side and back, pinned him against the wheel. Kassem surfaced fast, managed to get one hand on the track, watched as the tree actually started to rise, bark and branches tearing and splintering against the support cables. The trunk moved to a vertical position for an instant as the heavy roots swung under the bridge; ripping away from the truck, the crown plunged back into the current in a cascade of foam.

The tree passed under the bridge, branches scraping, surfaced immediately, resumed its momentum as it rolled downstream.

It had all happened in less than a minute. The bridge and truck were left tilted at a forty-five-degree angle. Badly shaken, Victor remained hunched over the wheel. He looked out through the tangle of branches still in the cab, saw Kassem cling to the track, throw one leg up, strain to climb back. The diesel was still chugging, windshield wipers moving, but Victor was aware of the severity of the angle; traction would be impossible. When Kassem was up on the track, he stood unsteadily for a moment, catching his breath, looking at Victor. He crouched as he moved to the front, studied the position of the wheels. Victor started removing branches from the cab; he felt pain in his side and back, touched the areas softly. His jacket was ripped, but he was too wet to tell if he was bleeding. It didn't matter. Nothing mattered, except that he was alive. When Kassem signaled him to accelerate, his arms and legs were shaking. He reacted slowly, mechanically, knowing it was useless. Kassem knew it, too, but wanted proof. Slowly, the wheels began to spin against the wood; the center of gravity was far too removed for traction.

Kassem watched, then remembered the

winch. He waved his arms quickly, telling Victor to stop, reached under the bumper, grabbed the hook, yanked out some slack, slung it over his shoulder, and stumbled ahead toward the bank, still crouched, not daring to run on the tilted tracks, pulling the cable behind him. He'd reached the end and was scrambling up the muddy bank toward the trees, when the bridge tilted several more degrees. Victor felt the truck begin to inch backward, just perceptibly, slammed his foot on the brake, but the motion continued. He was sliding back to the deeper water at a forty-seven-degree angle as Kassem struggled to get the cable around a tree. The instant he'd locked the hook, Kassem jumped away, yelling and waving his arms. Victor threw the winch into gear, braced himself, watched the cable lose slack quickly, then go taut and vibrate. He heard the gear grind, then catch. The backward motion stopped. No forward motion, and the cable was vibrating so badly that Victor thought it would either snap or the winch would break loose. On the bank, Kassem watched the palm tree lean; the cable loop jumped up a few inches, cutting deeply into the trunk.

Victor wasn't aware of movement until he heard the tires squeal against the steel siding. His arms and legs continued to shake. Kassem slid down the bank and ran for the bridge. As he watched the truck move toward him, tires squealing, he began crying, fighting it at first, almost instinctively, as he'd been taught all his life to do, then letting it happen, openly, luxuriously, as he ran out on the bridge, got up close and gave hand signals again, dimly aware that it was the first time he'd cried about anything since he was a child.

As the squealing diminished and the leveling began, Victor had to fight to keep the wheels on the tracks. The smell of burning rubber was replaced by burning metal as the winch reached its limits. With less than twenty-five feet to go, he touched the accelerator and got some traction. Not much, but enough to help. Ten feet. Almost level. Seven feet. Out of the water and level. Kassem stepped back on firm ground, staggered in the mud, got out of the way. Victor accelerated the last few feet, rolled off the bridge, turned off the key. He sat in silence, shaking, listening to rain drum on the roof.

13

REFLECTIONS OF TREE TRUNKS, still dark from the storm, rippled in the muddy stream that ran parallel to the road through the rest of the rain forest. At 12:30, the sun was just beginning to bake the road dry, and vapor steamed up from the moist dirt to blur the long rows of trees. Lazaro's odometer read ninety-one miles, and they were into the sixth hour. Jackie glanced at the "218" he'd chalked on the dash, *Above the buzz*, made a quick calculation. Only 127 miles to go, *above the rain*, and they were averaging about fifteen an hour. Fifteen into 127. Eight point four. Call it eight point five. Eight and a half hours to go. And just one more difficult section, "the grind," eight thousand feet up to the Paso al Infierno, into the clouds. After that, the road was supposed to be fairly decent all the way. He made a conscious effort to relax, *the sound of someone crying softly*, to stop squirming and massaging the wheel, *breathlessly*, to control the nervous jerking of his head *like a child*. But, from the moment he'd attacked Nilo, he knew something had happened to him. It wasn't like being drunk, it was like having a bad hangover, without a headache. Every muscle in his body felt tight. He was sweating so heavily that he had to wipe the palms of his hands constantly on his pants. Worst of all, he felt vaguely irrational, mouthing illogical words to himself, silently, repetitiously, *This is the wrong road!*, even though the detour had occurred more than three hours ago, and he knew by the map that he was back on the regular road—the only road—from Porvenir to Poza Rica. Nilo remained silent all the way, but his continual, soft, hacking cough irritated Jackie to the extent that he'd had to silently talk himself out of the very real compulsion to suddenly shove him out of the cab. But he needed Nilo. That's what really stopped him. If there was more trouble, he'd have to depend on the old man, like it or not. He needed him to survive.

The odometer read ninety-seven when Jackie maneuvered one of the long turns, and when he saw the obstruction in the road just half a mile ahead, his first reaction was blind anger, followed by a heightening sense of hysteria when he got closer and saw how bad it really was. A giant kaoba tree had fallen at an angle across the road, obviously struck by lightning that morning, because it was still fresh and green. As Jackie slowed and stopped, cursing, he felt blood rush to his head, began to see pinpoints of light.

Nilo got out first, walked around the cab, gazed up at it. The kaoba's trunk was approximately eight feet thick at the base, and its "flying buttress" roots extended at least eighteen feet, reaching above the road like a jagged abstract sculpture. Vines and parasitic plants clung to the bark. Nilo leaned against the fender, coughed, then started to laugh. It began as low, asthmatic, wheezing noises in his throat, gradually grew louder, higher, faster, as the absurd finality of the thing sunk in, until the laughter was uncontrollable. His legs gave out and he dropped to his knees almost gracefully, then down on his side, and the sounds turned into deep, helpless sobs.

Jackie walked up to the kaoba wide-eyed, glancing left and right. He waded into the gray-brown stream to the left, near the massive root structure, looking for a way around it, then came back, stumbled up on the road. Listening to Nilo's sobs, he squatted in the road, began punching the dirt with his right fist. Slowly at first, methodically, then getting into it, concentrating, left-right-left-right, fast combinations, then slower, harder each time, seeing the impressions of his knuckles, hearing the pleasant impacts, thud, thud, thud, thud, feeling the pain increase. He stopped when his fists became numb, crossed his arms over his chest, cradled the fists in his armpits, leaned over, rocked back and forth with the pain.

When he was aware of the jungle sounds again, hundreds of birds continuing their monotonous, oblivious, cheerful calls, and saw the splash of color around him, and smelled the heavy, rotting odors, he focused on Nilo, sitting hopelessly in the road, leaning back against the bumper. It infuriated him. He hadn't come this far *This is the wrong road!* to be defeated by a tree! He focused on the truck, *Where the hell're you going!* scrambled to his feet, ran to the cab, *We're gonna cross that bridge!* felt the energy pumping through him as he grabbed the two big machetes under the seat, ran back to the tree, splashed through the stream. Out of breath, arms shaking, he checked the trees around the kaoba roots. They were much smaller than the kaoba, looked skinny in comparison; he guessed their trunks to be from three to four feet thick. It would mean many hours of work, *Twenty thousand!* but they could do it, *'Cause I can't do it alone!* they still had a lot of daylight left. Cursing, he slashed at the undergrowth, splashed back across the stream.

Nilo was standing at the edge of the road, watching. He smiled sadly, shook his head. "You're crazy."

"*It's eight trees!*"

The old man laughed softly. "No way."

Jackie tossed a machete at his feet. "*Start chopping!*"

Without taking his eyes off Jackie, Nilo placed his right hand behind his back in a very deliberate motion. He became quite calm then, stood straight and ready. "Make your move."

Frowning, observing the instantaneous change, Jackie's respiration increased immediately. He stood completely still.

Nilo flicked up his shirt at the small of his back, reached in, removed the Mexican-manufactured Obregon .45 automatic from his belt, pointed it at Jackie's forehead. As he squeezed the trigger, he moved the barrel a fraction to the right, fired twice in rapid succession. Hearing the metal-jacketed slugs penetrate the tree, he smiled, watched Jackie's eyes, then fired a third time, laughed quietly.

Frozen in his position, shaking, feeling sweat run down his face, unable to see Nilo's eyes behind the dark glasses, Jackie heard the distant sound of what he recognized instantly as a diesel engine. Accelerating. Shifting up. Accelerating. Gradually, his breathing slowed. Keeping his eyes on Nilo, he backed away toward the road. Nilo took three slugs from his back pocket and reloaded.

Three minutes later, Victor took the wide turn, saw the huge tree, then the truck, then the men. He began shifting down at once, stopped slowly behind Lazaro.

Kassem stepped down from the running board, walked toward the tree with a bad limp; he'd twisted his left ankle in the fall from the bridge, but only became aware of it when the ordeal was over. Victor followed Jackie and Nilo into the stream to see the smaller trees. As he passed the jagged roots, Victor stopped, touched one.

"Kaoba," he told them. "Excellent wood."

Jackie pointed to the small trees; his voice was shrill: "It's only eight trees—we're going *through* it!"

"When you cut them down," Victor snapped, "how do you *move* them?"

"With the *winch!*"

"How you going to clear the *stumps?*" Nilo demanded. "How you going to drive through a *swamp!*"

"Impossible," Victor said.

"*Impossible?*" Jackie glared at them wide-eyed, turned, began splashing through the stream, swinging the machete wildly, hacking right and left at anything in his way, throat making painful sounds with every slash, stumbling on the rocks. Nilo took off his glasses, watched him with sad eyes. He'd seen other men in the same condition, too many, and he'd experienced it himself, many times, many years ago. It wasn't ordinary energy, or nervous energy, or desperate energy any more. It wasn't the energy of anger, or frustration, or aggression. It was something far more potent than a stimulant from the adrenal glands. It was the unmistakable energy of madness.

Victor watched, too, astonished at the sheer ferocity of the man, and the endurance, even though he'd seen it before, and felt it himself during combat. He went back up on the road.

Kassem was studying the kaoba trunk. He got a foothold in the vines, climbed up on it carefully, then limped along the thick bark, crouched slightly, examining the surface area that was free of parasites. He nodded several times, mouthing words to himself in Arabic, climbed down slowly, favoring his ankle.

Jackie finally stopped, his energy completely spent, and splashed out of the stream. Nilo continued to watch him carefully.

Kassem limped over to Victor, slapping dirt from his hands. "I think I can clear it."

* * *

Kassem gave very specific orders, didn't explain, the others didn't ask questions, just carried out the assignments exactly as told. Jackie selected a slender young tree, chopped it down, sliced off the crown, stripped the bark, carved a V-shaped notch in one end. Victor and Nilo found a long, straight branch on the kaoba, cut and stripped it, chopped it into three equal parts. Kassem spread a tarpaulin on the road in front of Sorcerer, dumped the contents of the truck's toolbox on it, began separating everything he'd need: heavy string, crowbar, wire, black electrical tape, four long nails, hammer, and his own switchblade.

When Victor gave Kassem the three lengths of wood, he wired them into a tripod. Returning the unnecessary tools to the box, he rolled the needed equipment in the tarpaulin, carried that and the tripod to the kaoba trunk, climbed carefully to the top. Victor and Nilo gathered various size rocks from the stream, climbed up the trunk, gave them to Kassem, who used two to brace the tripod. Jackie followed them up, delivered his slender tree. Kassem cradled it in the fork of the tripod, braced the low end with another rock. He ran the length of heavy string through the V-shaped notch at the high end, tied a small rock to it, lowered the rock halfway to the trunk, told Jackie to cut an X in the bark directly below the stone. After extending the string back to the tripod, he anchored it by placing a large rock in the fork, allowed about a foot of string to emerge from the rock, then cut the rest. Lastly, he selected the flattest rock of the bunch, placed it over the X cut, checked to be sure the dangling rock was precisely in line.

Kassem needed only a few other things. He searched the cabs of both trucks, found an empty Coke bottle under the driver's seat in Lazaro, and a small cloth bag in the glove compartment of Sorcerer. The other men stood in the road by the passenger side of Sorcerer as Kassem examined the bag.

"Too small," he said. He glanced at the men's trousers, pointed to Nilo's. "Show me your pockets."

Nilo hesitated, removed some coins, then turned both pockets inside-out.

Kassem snapped open his switchblade as he approached the man, inserted the point into the right-hand pocket, carefully carved it off. After inspecting the seam, he placed his hand inside, made a fist, and nodded. "Perfect."

He walked to the rear of the truck, removed the thick horizontal bolt on the left side of the tailgate, pointed to the right one. Victor unbolted it slowly. Cautiously, they inched the gate open. The hinges squeaked and stuck a bit; trickles of sawdust fell from both sides, then more, as the gate was lowered all the way. The supporting crosswires between the cases were still taut. Covered with sawdust, the three cases remained in the original triangular position. Kassem placed the white trouser pocket on the sawdust, used both hands to dig below to the layer of sand bedding. He scooped up handfuls of sand, filled the pocket to overflowing, squeezed off the top, limped back to the kaoba, climbed up quickly.

Jackie and Nilo were instructed to hack out a cavity in the kaoba, up near the incline of the roots, close to the flat rock. The explosives would be fitted into the cavity. Kassem wound a wire tightly around the top of the sand-filled pocket, closing it off. He squatted by the tripod, told Victor to hold the string taut before removing the rock in the tripod fork that anchored the string. Finally, he placed the pocket of sand where the rock had been. The pocket was heavy enough; the rock on the other end held.

On the way back to the truck, Kassem took a pair of wirecutters from the toolbox.

Jackie and Victor followed him around to the tailgate, while Nilo cleared an area on the kaoba where the case of nitro would temporarily be placed.

Since the triangular arrangement of the cases in Sorcerer had one case closest to the tailgate, Kassem had plenty of room to work. He lifted himself to kneel on the sawdust to the left of the case, leaned in to cut the supporting crosswires, bent them away, handed Victor the wirecutters. His face began to bead with sweat as he removed the sawdust from the top of the case, then the sides, to get a firm grip. With extreme care, he eased the case over the sand bedding toward the edge, where Jackie was ready to take it, hands braced, palms up, arms rigid. Jackie accepted it inch by inch, fingers under, palms against the sides, case moving into his stomach.

Before releasing his fingers, Kassem spoke softly, taking absolutely nothing for granted. His face was dripping then, almost touching Jackie's. "Got it?"

Jackie nodded.

Victor guided Jackie up the trunk. Each step was accomplished with deliberation, each foothold tested by Victor first. When they were directly over the place Nilo had cleared, they faced each other, Victor slid his fingers under the case until they touched

Jackie's, nodded when his grip was firm, and they both knelt, lifting slightly as they went down on one knee, then lowering it as they got the other knee down. When their fingers were flat on the bark, feeling the full weight, they gradually eased them out. Both men remained kneeling, taking deep breaths, before standing slowly and moving away.

Kassem slapped the crowbar in his palm as he limped over to the case. Kneeling beside it, he rubbed his left hand over the wood, looked closely at the underside of the lid, inserted the crowbar. The nails squeaked and groaned as he pried the lid up slowly, little by little, along one side only, fractions of inches, just enough to get his fingers under. He spread his knees, moved forward, held the sides of the case with the tips of his knees, lifted the lid with his fingertips. When the nails on that side were free, he slid his thumbs between them, pulled the lid back, twisted the remaining side off, placed the lid by his side. Before touching the thick polyethylene bag, he shook his hands to limber them up, rubbed his thumbs against his fingertips as he studied the position of the bag, rose to one knee. It was impossible to keep his hands from shaking when he reached inside, gripped the top, lifted the bag from the case. The long, fat brown sticks moved lower in the bag as he raised it. At the bottom was the urine-colored pool of nitroglycerin.

Nilo guided Kassem to the selected section of the elevated root structure, between the hacked-out cavity and the flat stone, where Jackie stood ready with the hammer and four nails. Kassem knelt, held the top of the bag against the thick bark, leaned to his right. Jackie crouched, positioned the first nail in the upper left corner, allowing enough of a margin for appreciable sag. He hesitated before hitting it, breathing hard, sweating, holding the other three nails in his mouth. The first blow gave him an indication of how thick the bark was. He drove it all the way in with four more hard swings, winced each time. Kassem nodded, sweat dripping, leaned to the left as far as he could. Jackie went around him, positioned the second nail in the upper right corner. Five hard strokes. All the way in. Kassem stayed in that position, ducked his head. Jackie stood over him, slammed in the other two nails along the top, equidistant from the first two, then stepped away.

Kassem raised his head, looked at the nails, kept his eyes on them as he began to release his grip at the sides, very slowly. The bag strained against the nails, but held. He removed his hands, wiped the sweaty palms on his jeans, stood up, began shaking his fingers to regain full circulation. Victor handed him the empty Coke bottle.

Kassem spoke quietly. "Get the rope now."

As Victor went back to the truck for the ten-foot rope, Kassem walked to the tarpaulin, picked up the roll of black electrical tape, tore off one long and one short strip, attached them to his right sleeve at the elbow. On his way back to the polyethylene bag, he used the side of his foot to gently kick the empty nitro case off the tree. When it bounced against the side of the trunk, he was momentarily startled to see a large bird take flight from the parasitic plants; Jackie and Nilo stepped back involuntarily when they saw the size of it. Victor, walking toward the tree, had the best view, and recognized it instantly when he saw its bald head and huge wingspan. It was an Andean condor, common to Chile, and widely known as the largest vulture in the Western Hemisphere. Its wings fluttered wildly at first, then slower and more gracefully as the frightened creature gained altitude.

Kassem went back to work, knelt by the polyethylene bag, studied the two bottom corners, yellow with the liquid nitro. The bag hung with a slight sag to the left. He touched the very edge of that corner, where a tiny nipple had formed. When he took out his switchblade and clicked it open, he held it in front of him for a moment, loosely, then tightly, to see how much his hand trembled. He picked up the Coke bottle in his left hand, held it against the nipple, touched the nipple with the point of the blade, pressed gently. As the yellow liquid began to trickle, he dropped the knife, held the bottle with both hands until it was approximately one-quarter full. He pinched off the flow with his right thumb and forefinger, carefully set the bottle down, peeled the short strip of tape from his right sleeve, and wrapped it tightly around the nipple, including his fingertips. When he withdrew his fingers, he massaged the tape until no more bubbles appeared. He stared at the tape as he wiped his fingers dry, stood up slowly, removed the long strip of tape from his sleeve, wrapped it around the top of the bag, just below the four nails. Turning to Victor, he took the ten-foot rope, tied it loosely around the top of the bag, about one inch below the tape, both ends approximately even, then began tightening it slowly. He tied the final knot, stood. Jackie and Nilo took their positions in the hacked-out cavity on the root elevation, about three feet above him. They leaned over as he handed each of them one end of the rope.

"Ready?" he asked.

They moved several feet apart, pulled

their ends taut, adjusted their positions, glanced at each other. Both gave nods.

Kassem slowly cut the bag away from the nails, held its sides for a moment as they lifted it, gently, up the three-foot incline, and lowered it into the cavity. He signalled all of them to get back to the trucks. The rest was his.

When they were gone, he rubbed his hands on his jeans again, knelt beside the Coke bottle. The yellow liquid caught the sun, glistened, as he picked it up in both hands, turned, moved on his knees to the flat stone nearby. He placed it in the middle, glanced at the rock dangling above his head, then got down on his back, face near the bottle, sweating, trying to judge the angle of fall. When he heard the engines start, shift, and begin to back up, he stood, picked up one of the larger rocks Victor and Nilo had found, knelt once more, tilted the bottle against the rock, offering a wider target. He made certain the bottle was firm before standing and limping to the tripod.

He glanced at the trucks as they retreated along the road, Sorcerer way back already, at least a quarter mile away, Lazaro going slower, waiting for him, and he tried to imagine Nilo's expression. Then, with a series of gestures that just missed being grand, he took out his knife, clicked the blade open, crouched by the tripod, and moved the point to the underside of the white, sand-filled pocket. He touched it, twisted slowly, felt it give. The trickle of sand sparkled for an instant, *a single fly* made a soft hissing sound as it *buzzed loudly* fell to the bark below.

Rising and pivoting in a single motion, Kassem took several wide, light strides, as if in a walking race, climbed down the trunk, and ran, limping painfully, for Lazaro in the shimmering distance. Feeling the massive rush of adrenaline, hearing his throat make sounds with every step, realizing suddenly that he'd never make it to the truck, *bars of orange-yellow light* it was stimulating beyond belief, *played across the foot of the bed*, terrifying beyond belief, *rippled to the contours* the ultimate sensory experience, *of a faded blue quilt* the ultimate trip, to know that death could be *a single fly* that death could be *buzzed loudly* that death could be *around the ceiling* less than ten seconds *batted against* less than five seconds *the window slats* less than a second away.

14

In the split second between flash and deafening sound, trees flanking the road were bent by shock waves, then instantly sucked into the partial vacuum, then snapped back as the enormous red ball billowed up. Victor and Nilo, backing around the wide curve half a mile from the blast, felt the truck sway, looked up to see a blurred shower of debris emerge from thick black smoke, tumble high in the air, ricochet against the crowns of the trees. The explosion echoed loudly through the near mountains, reechoed from the more distant. Lighter fragments of wood began floating down, spraying the trees, then leaves drifted gracefully, followed by a gentle snowfall of white ash, as the echoes softened. Still holding his ears, Victor wasn't at all certain he hadn't heard two almost simultaneous explosions. He took his hands away, heard distant murmurs, glanced at Nilo, who stared straight ahead. White ash began building on the windshield. Victor leaned out, wiped it with his left hand, then Nilo wiped the other side. As he shifted and touched the accelerator, Victor experienced a mounting suspicion that the two of them might very well be alone now.

Rounding the curve slowly, they saw Lazaro in the middle of the road. Like everything else in the area, it was covered with chunks of wood, leaves, and white ash. In the distance, the kaoba had virtually vanished. Ash was still falling in that area, but they could see a large and apparently shallow declivity in the road, littered with hundreds of small white mounds; on both sides of the road, a scorched and jagged semicircle had been ripped into the tangle of trees. Smoke hung in layers, and there was a sharp smell of powder. Victor drove cautiously, watching for large pieces of wood and rock.

As they approached Lazaro, they saw Kassem leaning against the front fender of the driver's side, rubbing his hair. Then Jackie swung out of the cab, began wiping the windshield with a rag. Victor pulled around to the left and stopped. Nilo climbed out, discovered that his legs were shaking, steadied himself on the fender. When he looked down the road, he saw a single condor circling the high drift of smoke and ash, wings spread wide and motionless, gliding slowly.

Victor leaned over, called to Jackie. "You all right?"

He shook the rag. "Yeah, I'm okay."

Kassem climbed in, glanced at Victor with a slight smile. They watched Jackie finish the windshield. His hair was speckled gray-white. He shook the rag again, then sat back in the cab.

"If you have no objections," Victor told him, "we'll go on ahead."

Jackie nodded. "Hang loose."

❀ ❀ ❀

It looked relatively low from the rain forest, more like an oversized foothill than a mountain, nowhere near eight thousand feet, despite the presence of cumulonimbus clouds that concealed its summit. Just minutes before they started the climb, Victor became aware of the optical illusion created by distance. Only one feature gave it true dimensional perspective: the angular, geometric meandering of the road, gray in sunlight, climbing with countless switchbacks that became extremely narrow zigzag patterns before entering the clouds. At the first substantial incline, the road became gravel, and Victor shifted up one gear as soon as he heard the welcome sound of crunching; at least he wouldn't have to worry about holes. What had looked like boulders from a distance of only a few miles turned out to be massive granite walls draped with bright green Spanish moss. He slowed when he reached the first turn, picked up some speed before the next. Within fifteen minutes, he began to realize why it took so long to climb: the turns became progressively more frequent as the angle of ascent increased.

The really difficult part didn't begin until they'd reached the elevation where the clouds began. All color started to become muted, and forms appeared and vanished abruptly, swirling across the road like wind-blown fog. As it became dense and constant, moisture formed on the windshield. Victor turned on the wipers, then the fog lights. He slowed to fifteen between the turns, then twelve, then ten. Finally, he put it in compound low, tried to relax some, but couldn't. He began to feel disoriented; he could barely see the road.

During the next half hour, the clouds broke up periodically for short intervals, and he could see stretches of the road and the solid rock wall to his left. Partly to take advantage of those times, partly to keep himself alert, he shifted up as he rounded the curves, then down when he neared another.

Despite the bad visibility, he felt himself getting into the rhythm of the road. One long period of very heavy clouds was followed by partial clearing, and, as he hugged the rock wall on a turn and shifted up, he caught a glimpse of the summit. It was blurred in an instant, but he was positive he'd seen it. They were nearly there; going down would be much easier. He was tempted to glance at his watch, but kept his eyes on the road, certain it couldn't be much longer.

After navigating an unusually long curve and emerging from two thick sections of cloud, he could feel the road start to level. The rock wall was gone, replaced by a hill with a few trees. More clouds drifted past. On the left side of the road near the hill, a small cluster of glass and metal objects glistened in the fog lights. As he pulled closer, he could make out a small altar constructed of rocks, holding old headlights, various large medals, and a row of wooden crosses, obviously meant to indicate the Paso al Infierno. He smiled, remembering his discussion with Corlette: *Even the police won't anger the spirits of the road by hauling explosives over the Paso al Infierno. The stupid are also superstitious.*

Squinting at what gravel he could see, he took out his cigarettes, lit one quickly, held out the pack.

Kassem declined with a wave of his hand, spoke quietly. "Are you from Paris?"

"I lived there, yes."

"Where?"

"Seizième arrondissement. Do you know Paris?"

"I was there for two days. It's very expensive."

"So they say."

"Your family is there?"

"My wife. Just my wife."

"No children?"

"No children." Caught by the memory, Victor took a drag, inhaled very deeply, then reached down, felt for the ashtray, stubbed out the new cigarette. "I met my wife when I first came to Paris from Bretagne." He reached into his breast pocket, took out the gold watch, handed it to Kassem. "The day she gave me this watch was the last day I saw her."

Kassem examined it, turned it over, read the inscription.

As they started the descent, Victor shifted down, squinting. It was moderately steep. When gravity took over, he touched the brake several times, testing. Kassem handed him the watch. He took a quick look, put it back in his pocket. "It's five minutes before nine in Paris."

He didn't hear the rifle, just the sudden loud blast of the right front tire as it exploded. It collapsed instantly on the rim, the cab dipped low to the right, then shook violently as the bumper hit the road, sending up a wake of gravel and sparks. Victor slammed on the emergency air brake. Skidding, vibrating, tires burning and squealing, Sorcerer skidded to the edge of the road, nearly stopped, then lunged over. It exploded in midair.

*　*　*

Lazaro was parked on the road 1,500 feet below, and Jackie was pouring water into the steaming radiator. The explosion was so loud that he and Nilo crouched and froze. They looked at each other through the heavy mist. The echoes and reverberations were painfully loud, like close thunder, moving through the mountains for almost a full minute, replaced by the gathering volume of a small landslide. They turned and watched silently as earth and rocks tumbled down the stone wall to their left, pale orange in the fog lights, and piled up in the road. When the echoes were gone, Jackie forced himself to pour the remaining water into the radiator, used a rag to screw on the hot cap, motioned

Nilo to get in. He maneuvered around the big pile of earth, rolled slowly over rocks scattered across the width of the road. It was the same all the way to the summit.

The smell of powder and burning rubber became progressively stronger as they rounded the long turn leading up to the Paso al Infierno, but the clouds were so thick that Jackie had no idea of where he was until he felt the road begin to level. Before he reached the altar, the clouds broke, then swirled past thickly again. He kept his eyes on the gravel, didn't see the altar at all, shifted down and slowed when he began the descent. Then the smell of burning rubber became almost sickening. The fog lights picked up a long strangely shaped object to the left. Jackie squinted at it, foot on the brake, as he inched downward. It was the rear axle of Sorcerer, jagged strips of rubber still smoldering, hanging like tar from the rims. When he drove around it, he made a conscious effort not to look directly at it, just its black form. Only seconds later, he had to stop. The road was completely littered by the blast. Large and small chunks of twisted metal and glass sparkled in the fog lights. The stench was virtually unbearable. Nilo began coughing in short, soft, baby-like spasms, which he tried to stifle when Jackie shut off the engine.

They sat in silence, watched the clouds drift past gleaming objects, orange in the fog lights. Nilo held his hand over his mouth and nose. Jackie took a deep breath, another, climbed out, then held on to the fender, not wanting to see any more. But he couldn't risk driving through it. He'd have to physically pick up the larger debris, no matter what it was, to clear a safe path. He felt sick to his stomach. His hands and legs shook as he stepped away and moved ahead into the orange light.

He stopped when he heard footsteps. Slow, crunching sounds at first, from the right side of the road, then the left. He caught only a glimpse of them in the mist. Both held submachine guns. As they walked toward him and into the fog lights, Jackie stood perfectly still, hands by his sides. The one on the left, who looked to be in his mid-twenties, had a high forehead and deep-set eyes; the other was even younger, with very scholarly, severe features. A third man came down the hill quickly and into the light, young and well-built; his short-sleeved shirt revealed muscular arms. All three kept their guns trained on Jackie, but looked at the man walking up behind him.

Manuel Medina approached quickly, motioned for the others to spread out. He was thirty-two, long-haired, with a bushy mustache. As one of three aide-de-camps to Salvador Allende from 1970 until the coup of 1973, he'd developed an easy air of authority that left no doubt about who was in charge.

He looked Jackie up and down. "*No te mueves. A rodillas.*"

"*No comprendo.*"

"Get down!" Medina snapped. He turned to Teru, the muscular man who was his second-in-command. "*Saces el otro del camión.*" Then, to Jackie: "Get *down!* On the *ground!*"

Jackie got on his knees, as Teru went to the cab and began shouting at Nilo.

Medina held the submachine gun in his right hand, reached out with the left, removed Jackie's fedora, put it on. "What you have in the truck?"

"Supplies."

"For what, supplies?"

"Vienna sausages, Wonder Bread, Northern Tissue . . ."

Medina smiled, grabbed Jackie's shoulder, pulled him up, then shoved him back toward the truck. "Nothing else?"

Jackie shrugged, moved toward the rear of the truck, glanced in at Nilo, who was into a coughing spasm. Teru was still yelling at

248

him in Spanish, prodding him with a sten gun, but he wasn't moving. When Jackie reached the tailgate, he was surrounded by three of the four men.

Medina grinned at the others. "He says this truck is carrying groceries."

The scholarly kid laughed loudly; the one with deep-set eyes just smiled, shook his head.

"Okay," Medina told Jackie. "So, you just got what we need. You don't have to be afraid from us."

Teru stopped yelling at Nilo, called back: "*Es un loco!*"

Smiling, Medina stepped to the side, looked at Nilo in the big side-view mirror, then spoke to Jackie. "What he has?"

"His mother was in the other truck."

Medina touched the end of his mustache, laughed softly, looked at the other men again. "This gringo is very funny." He prodded Jackie with the gun, moved him up the passenger side of the cab, called to Nilo: "Listen, amigo, just come out. We just need this truck. We just need food, you know?" He glanced at Jackie. "And toilet paper."

Nilo coughed, raised his voice. "*Enfermo.*"

When Medina shoved him against the truck, Jackie's left hand felt the shovel that was clamped to the side. He leaned against it, gripped the handle, watched Nilo's bald pate in the long side-view mirror. He was doubled up, coughing, coat in his lap.

Medina frowned at the old man, stepped up on the running board, leaned in, paused a moment as he looked through the rear window of the cab. He pursed his lips, glanced down at Teru. *"Hay un montón de explosivos."* When he turned to face Nilo, his eyes almost focused on the barrel of the Obregon .45 before his brains exploded from the back of his skull. Nilo instantly shot the scholarly kid to his left. Teru fired a wild volley before Jackie slammed the shovel into his neck, but the man with deep-set eyes sprayed at least a dozen shots directly into the cab, knocking Nilo back against the dash. As he bounced forward, holding the gun in both hands, he fired twice, hitting the man in the chest and neck, then fired again as he fell out. Jackie stood over Teru, pounding him with the shovel. Already unconscious, Teru made low sounds in his throat each time the shovel landed, again and again. Nilo rolled over, braced himself on his elbows, aimed carefully at Teru's temple, squeezed off a final shot.

In the silence, Jackie stood poised with the shovel over his head, ready to hit anything that moved. Clouds swirled on the road, obscuring Nilo for a moment; he braced himself into a half-sitting position and looked at his legs. When he saw blood pumping through his trousers, he screamed. Jackie dropped the shovel, stumbled over to him. They faced each other for a moment, breathing hard, then Jackie moved behind him, gripped under his arms, dragged him up to the running board. Nilo sat on it, leaned back, coughing, beginning to cry with pain. Jackie climbed in, sat down, grabbed under his arms again, used all his strength to pull the old man up, but couldn't get him on the seat.

Crying softly on the floor, twisting, Nilo looked down at the road, stared at the vermilion liquid starting to move through the gravel. At first he thought he was hallucinating: It moved down the steep grade swiftly then, a stream of it, several streams meeting, dark and thick, flowing over and around shattered glass, twisted metal, broken fog lights, fragments of mirrors, gained more momentum as streams converged, splashing, curving, quivering, rushing, reaching out in multiple rivulets; over and around objects from the young men's pockets—keys, coins, a gold wristwatch; over and around debris of his own—a pack of cigarettes, sunglasses, a dust-covered doll.

Behind the wheel, out of breath, Jackie squinted ahead as he turned the key and revved the engine. He'd maneuver through the wreckage, stop only if he had no other choice. Shaking, he pulled the knob to release the air brake, shifted to compound low, moved slowly down the steep incline in the mist. The truck swayed as it rolled over large chunks of debris.

Nilo coughed, tasted blood, struggled for breath as he experienced a surge of pain. "The whole thing's down the drain."

"You're full of shit." Jackie eased around a heavy object; it scraped loudly against the entire length of the truck. "What're you going to do with all that bread, you hump?" He waited, eyes on the road. "Talk to me. What're you—"

"Get laid."

"Huh?" Jackie glanced at him, laughed softly, then all-out.

Nilo coughed, smiled. "Best whore in Managua."

"*Two* whores!" Jackie laughed in a high, hysterical way, trying to visualize it. "The two best whores in Managua!"

They were clear of the wreckage, heading down a relatively smooth section of road, when Nilo began coughing up blood. He spoke with difficulty. "You do it, kid."

"Huh?"

"Do it for me."

Jackie shook his head. "*With* you, man."

He coughed, spat blood on the floor. "You do it. For me. Okay?"

Jackie hesitated. "Okay."

"No bullshit?"

"I'll do it."

Nilo nodded, seemed to relax then, to enter a state of reverie, as if the most important matter had been resolved. A promise.

They drove in silence, except for the bang of the muffler, taking the curves slowly. In less than half an hour, they were out of the clouds, with good visibility, and Jackie couldn't help glancing down frequently at the bizarre landscape of the Culo del Diablo in the distance, its twisting canyons taking deep primary colors in the late afternoon. The enormous, isolated, flat-topped mesas and buttes looked like tiny red and yellow rocks, but threw long shadows. Beyond, the tall column of black smoke seemed small, too, bent by the wind, leaning like the silhouette of a palm tree.

Nilo, staring fixedly up at the seat, drifting calmly into unconsciousness, thought about Agrippa, her unassuming manner, her quiet voice, the opacity of her eyes, the simplicity of her life and her faith. "God's old lady," he told himself.

"What?"

"Jackie?"

"Yeah, it's all right."

"Kiss her on the mouth." He laughed softly, coughed. The face of Agrippa receded to an infinity of faces that seemed to blur now, then pulsate to the fast rhythms of muffler bang and tire whine, a simultaneous combination of dreamlike, cacophonous tones, at unrest, needing completion. His body collapsed into its clothing as it began the process of ceasing to be alive.

Darkness seemed to come quickly in the long shadow of the mountain, and the element that bothered Jackie most was his increasingly confused state of mind. It intensified when he entered the Culo del Diablo. The world outside the cab became totally unreal in the headlights. A large swarm of fireflies, blinded by the lights, spattered across the windshield, causing the landscape and road and horizon to become splintered and abstract, but he was incapable of stopping, even for a minute, in those dark canyons. Isolated mesas and buttes that had looked so small from the mountain now assumed their gigantic dimensions, perpendicular sides towering black above an extraterrestrial plateau. Wind currents became unpredictable, whipping through the cab from various angles, stinging his eyes with sand. An overwhelming, sickening visu-

al and aural sensation kept recurring rhyth-
mically, fragments from a familiar dream,
giving him the vague, dizzy, subliminal
awareness that he'd experienced all this
before, knew exactly what would happen
next, was powerless to stop it. What looked
like a typical sixteenth-century Spanish galleon *You know whose parish this is?* seemed
to have either run aground on fog-shrouded
rocks *You're dead* or was half-buried on the
bottom of the sea, *You're all dead* he could
never be certain *Thin layers of smoke hanging near the table*, The square-rigged sails
and beyond, in the corner, on its three masts
three priests standing close together, were
billowing in a raging storm *hands around
the steampipe*, or underwater current, *and
the old one sitting on the floor* then started
to rip apart, *I heard faint organ music*, then
shred, *the happy kind they play* the high
bow and stern listing, straining *at the end of
weddings* The sound had changed from wind
and water *I could smell smoke on his coat*
to a distorted chorus of bell frogs *Above the
buzz, above the rain*, combined with the
steady, unrelenting, *the sound of someone
crying softly* mechanical drone *He was trying to say something*, of unseen legions of
insects *but his mouth was pressed against
the dash* The scream of a pig *I felt warm
blood on my hands, yanked them back* from

the slaughterhouse down by the river *Where am I going?* Get a train down to Baltimore *Where am I going?* I owed you a favor and this is it *Where am I going?*

The shrill, piercing sound of the radiator cap, and the muffler banging louder than he'd ever heard one. He looked at the heat gauge: the dial was as far into the red danger area as it would go. Shaking his head quickly, blinking, he shifted down, pulled over, stopped, turned off the engine, but left the lights on. Sweating, feeling his heart pound, he walked around the cab, pulled Nilo's body as gently as he could, dragged it across the road to the base of a mesa, propped it in a sitting position. He turned away quickly, didn't look back until he was seated in the cab. In the soft periphery glow of all the lights on the top and front of the cab, the old man's figure was dwarfed by the steep sides of the mesa, and diminished to a white speck by the enormous horizon of mountains that had dominated that land for millions of years, and would continue to do so for unimaginable millions more: calm, cold, quiet, massive, benignly indifferent to brief little creatures and their frightened little lives.

The high scream continued. Jackie turned the key, pressed the accelerator. The engine wouldn't start. He floored it, let up easily.

No good. After several more attempts, he tried it with the throttle. No good. The knob finally broke off. He threw it away, glanced at the odometer: 216. Two miles to go. Drawing very deep breaths, he climbed down and walked mechanically along the dark road to the tailgate. The sickening sensation was still there.

When he walked past the cab and into the first shaft of bright yellow light, his shadow jumped far ahead in the dirt road, then split in two, then fractured into seven with the lights on top, each shadow a different shade, bouncing a little with every step. The radiator cap was still screaming, but in spurts now, rapid, almost rhythmic, breathless, like a hurt animal. The shadows faded, one by one, step by step, and the road became dark. It took much longer for the little screams to stop, but they did, minute by minute, softer, lower, gone. Only his footsteps remained. Heavy in the dirt, slow, stumbling sometimes. No moonlight, no stars, just the blurred outlines of the road, black mesas against heavy clouds, and the mountains, dominating.

The burning oil well looked like he knew it would. It looked like a spark, from a mile and a half. From a mile, it looked like the flame of a match, flickering. From three thousand feet, it looked like a candle, wavering. From two thousand feet, it looked like a red geyser, splashing. From the front gate, it looked like the eruption of a volcano, and sounded like it, and felt like it, as he carried the case of nitro inside.

15

Tuesday morning, January 24, the Mariette 1 oil field held vast pools of melted foam, pale yellow in the sun, steaming, distorting the dark skeletal reflections of the four remaining derricks. Long lengths of high-pressure hoses lay deserted, half submerged, slick with black mud, twisted, crisscrossed, like scaly hulks of Cenozoic pythons, and the smell of chemicals was very strong, particularly hydrogen chloride. Although Corlette had teletyped COREPET headquarters at 12:57 a.m., less than twenty minutes after the fire was blown out, the reply didn't reach his office until 8:32, just minutes before he left for Porvenir. He ripped it off the machine, glanced at it as he trudged across the field with Mort Cooper and Bobby Del Ríos, but his eyes began watering from the chemical stench. When they reached Billy White's roaring helicopter at the edge of the field, he shoved the message in his pocket, shouted final instructions to Cooper, and climbed in. Jackie, sitting in the back with Zayas, looked fairly rested, despite his irritated eyes. He'd slept for seven hours, uninterrupted except for the explosion at 12:36, showered and shaved, had two cups of black coffee, and Corlette had loaned him a clean blue shirt, dark trousers, a white sports jacket, and even a good-looking fedora. They were all a little big for him, but not by much. He looked strangely out of place, sitting next to Zayas in his denim work clothes, like a small-town salesman, or a tourist.

Corlette waited until they were airborne before taking out the message. He had to hold it in both hands because of the strong vibrations.

HQ 1-24 0832
CORLETTE CHIEF OPER POZA RICA
TRUST CANNOT BE BASED ON THE FEAR THAT OUR TRUST WILL BE BETRAYED. CONGRATULATIONS EXTINGUISHMENT. REGRET LOSS OF LIFE CONSULTANTS.

DERRICK CONSTRUCTION DEADLINE 2-1 REPEAT 2-1. OVERTIME AUTHORIZED UNDER FOLLOW-

ING SCHEDULE. EFFECTIVE IM-
MEDIATELY CMA ALL MARIETTE
1 NON-MANAGEMENT EMPLOY-
EES ELIGIBLE DOUBLE-TIME
RATE ALL HOURS EXCEEDING
EIGHT PER WEEKDAY CMA PER
COREPET REG. 538-2 CMA PLUS
BONUS DOUBLE-TIME RATE ALL
EIGHT-HOUR DAYS WORKED
WEEKENDS CMA PER COREPET
REG. 538-3.

EFFECTIVE 0900 WEDNESDAY
CMA ALL NON-MANAGEMENT
REFINERY EMPLOYEES RE-
TURNED TO PAYROLL. REIN-
FORCE PROMISE MADE MANAGE-
MENT/SPECIALIST EMPLOYEES
1-20 CMA 3 PERCENT REPEAT 3
PERCENT GENERAL SALARY AD-
JUSTMENT EFFECTIVE 3-1 CMA
PROVIDED NEW DEADLINE OF
2-28 ACHIEVED RE YOUR 160
THOUSAND BARRELS.

LARTIGUE INFORMED RE ISSU-
ANCE APPROVAL CERTIFIED
CHECK CMA AMOUNT $40 THOU-
SAND REPEAT $40 THOUSAND
CMA ORDER JUAN DOMINGUEZ.
CHILEAN GOVERNMENT

SOURCES NOTIFIED DOCUMEN-
TATION REQUIREMENTS CMA
CONFIRM ISSUANCE VIA LAR-
TIGUE 0700. DOMINGUEZ TRANS-
PORTATION VIA DC-3 CHARTER
ARRANGED CMA ETA PORVENIR
1100 CMA ETA BONAO 1530. LEF-
FERTS AIRPORT CONTACT. CORE-
PET BANK NOTIFIED STANDBY
CASH TRANSACTION. END.
                          —WEBBER.

*   *   *

At nine o'clock that morning, all regularly
scheduled radio programs aired in southern
Chile were preceded by a special announcement from President Ignacio Lopez Guitierrez, and read live by presidential press
secretary Emilio Alvarado:

"As a result of the patriotism and courage
of the workers of Porvenir, the unfortunate
fire at the COREPET oil field was extin-
guished early this morning. COREPET officials are happy to announce that full
employment will be restored tomorrow morning, and workers will be eligible for overtime
wages at double the standard rate for the
next five weeks to help improve the economy.

"Success was achieved, without loss of life,

through the diligence and determination of our combined efforts, but one citizen deserves our special commendation, worker Juan Dominguez, who risked his life in pursuit of our common trust. Civil and military authorities will accord Señor Dominguez the welcome of a proud and grateful nation when he arrives in Porvenir this morning, before leaving on a paid holiday in Bonao. Congratulations to all on a job well done."

❉　❉　❉

The smell of rain was unusually strong in Porvenir at 9:30, and puddles in the main street shimmered in the breeze, blurring the images of workers and their families in the long, slow, silent procession to the square. Past the slaughterhouse by the river, where small wood fires still burned; past the narrow alleys, where more families emerged; past La Paloma Dulce, where young workers leaned out the windows; past the angular shadows of corrugated shacks and huts leading to the muddy square, where soldiers were scrubbing the large horizontal poster holding two rows of four identical photographs, all of President Ignacio Lopez Guitierrez. The two burned-out trucks had already been removed; four deep gouges extended up the length of the square toward the road to the town dump, where the trucks had been dragged on their back rims. The COREPET Jeep that would take Jackie to El Corsario with Corlette and Zayas, after a stop at the refinery, was not due for another hour, but the local police car was parked in front of the veranda, and the two officers were in the *taberna*, waiting.

In the room Nilo had occupied, Carlos was disposing of the man's belongings, as Lartigue had directed. There wasn't much in the battered dresser, a few sport shirts, underwear, socks, handkerchiefs, and, on the table near the sink, toothbrush and paste, comb, an aerosal can of shaving cream, an old straight razor, some small bottles of medicine. He found the photograph in an inside pocket of the leather valise. It was a very formal black-and-white portrait, a little frayed at the edges, but not cracked. The young man who looked out at him from a distance of thirty-four years wore the familiar, handsomely tailored dress uniform of a Nazi SS lieutenant. Fair-haired, fair-skinned, muscular, his shoulders were thrown back, and the smiling face had a proud lift to the chin. It didn't resemble Marquez in the slightest, except for the eyes. Beyond question, they were his. Carlos took a last look at the proud young man, then tore the picture into very small pieces, dropped them out the back window, and moved on to Victor's room.

*　*　*

When Jackie arrived in the square at 10:25, a crowd of more than three hundred people gave him a tumultuous welcome, dozens running alongside the Jeep, trying to shake his hand, pounding Corlette and Zayas on the back, and the vehicle was surrounded when it stopped next to the police car in front of El Corsario. Drums normally played at voodoo ceremonies began their loud, frenzied rhythms, triggering immediate dancing, mostly by children, then teenage boys started drumming on the hood of the Jeep, following the fast tempo. As the three men were beginning to wonder how they'd get out and into the *taberna*, the sad-eyed policeman walked down the steps with the athletic-looking officer, pushed the crowd back with nightsticks, and gradually escorted the men inside.

Jackie took a table near the bar with Corlette and Zayas. Agrippa served them coffee immediately. The policemen selected a table near the door; both watched Jackie attentively. Corlette took out the manila envelope Lartigue had given him, opened it, removed the certified check in the amount of $40,000, and a national passport.

He handed Jackie the check. "It's good."

Jackie held a cigarette in his mouth as he examined it. "No good to me." He lit the cigarette quickly, blew out the match. "What do I do with this, take it into a bank, flash an I.D., and give 'em a thumbprint? Our deal was cash."

Corlette shook his head. "Our head office is sending a man by the name of Gus Lefferts to meet you at the plane. He'll take you to our bank, you'll have that cashed by supper-time." He glanced at the red-yellow-black passport, gave it to Jackie. "You might ask Lefferts when you see him what's available in the capital." He took out a cigarette, lit it. "I told him you were a first-rate driver."

"Not any more."

Corlette smiled, blew out the match. "Well, if you find anything that's good, send me a postcard, and maybe I'll join you."

"You mean you'd give all this up?"

"Six months' time, who knows? I may not have any choice." He picked up his coffee, changed his mind, put it down, turned to the bar. "Carlos? *Traega nos tres cervezas, por favor.*" After pushing his cup away, he looked at Jackie, spoke softly. "You know, there's one place down here that—might be kind of nice for a guy in your situation. You ever think of going to Managua?"

"Managua?" Jackie glanced down and away, remembering his promise. "Shit, there's no way I can go to Managua."

"Too bad. It's a nice place."

"No," he said very softly. "Managua's no good for me."

Agrippa padded over with the three beers, wearing her black dress again. She served Jackie first, smiled at him. Two workmen came in, walked to the bar, nodded to Carlos. Outside, the drums had stopped, and the crowd noises were softening.

Corlette watched Jackie drink the beer. "How about a chaser?" Without waiting for an answer, he stood up, went to the bar. "Carlos?"

"*Haben Scotch*," Carlos told him.

As Corlette carried the bottle and three glasses back to the table, Carlos switched on the ancient radio, moved the dial through a series of Spanish newscasts, then merengue music, stopped when he heard something that sounded American. It was Charlie Parker's recording of "I'll Remember April."

Corlette sat down, began to pour, paused to reach in his back pocket. "Oh, by the way." He took out a sealed white envelope, handed it to Jackie. "When you get into Bonao, would you mail that for me?"

Nodding automatically, Jackie took it, glanced at the name and address:

> Mme. B. Manzon
> 88 Ave. Foch
> Paris, France

Jackie put the envelope in the breast pocket of his jacket, watched Agrippa move carelessly in time with the slow jazz. In a few seconds, she was dancing in place, arms and legs moving gracefully, dark hair swirling. She danced in an almost stationary shuffle, knees bent slightly, arms in close and pumping softly, as if trying to walk with her feet glued to the floor. The two workmen at the bar nudged each other, laughed, made a few comments. Agrippa closed her eyes, oblivious to them, really feeling the music. Jackie sipped the Scotch, stared at the floor, remembering his other promise.

He turned to Corlette. "Have a couple of minutes?"

"For you, they'll hold the plane."

He stood, walked slowly to Agrippa. She tossed back her hair, smiled warmly, continued to dance in place.

"May I have this dance?"

Shyly, tenderly, she moved into his arms,

and Jackie was gently, if a bit awkward, holding her close, as they stepped lightly, slowly, turning, again and again. The laughter stopped. Every man in the room, even the police officers, stared openly, remembering.

Outside, most of the crowd had dispersed, but a few workers stood at the door, watching, listening to the soft saxophone. The only vehicle moving on the street was the beat-up 1963 Chevrolet with the word TAXI badly hand-painted on the door, arriving from the airport. It bounced and squeaked, splashing through the puddles, entered the square slowly, stopped near the veranda of El Corsario.

After the driver was paid, the first passenger stepped out. His shoes were white, well-polished, expensive, the gray suit was almost unwrinkled, and the yellow shirt was open at the neck. His short mustache was dark, and would have dominated the expressionless face, but for the eyes. They were as cold as ever, like brown glass. He waited for his companion, an older man, equally well-dressed in a light blue suit, white silk sport shirt, white shoes. It had been a long journey, *He robbed my church* but the two men didn't look at all tired. On the contrary, *He shot my brother* they appeared cool and refreshed, *I want his ass* looking forward to

269

the schedule of events *I don't care where he
is* that only a meticulously planned *I want
him dead* and professionally executed military operation could hope to achieve. Vinnie
Reggio and his companion walked slowly
inside.

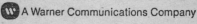